NESTING

NESTING

Short Stories

David Almond

First published 2013 by IRON Press
5 Marden Terrace
Cullercoats
North Shields
NE30 4PD
tel/fax +44(0)191 2531901
ironpress@blueyonder.co.uk
www.ironpress.co.uk

ISBN 978-0-9565725-7-8
Printed by Field Print Ltd
Boldon on Tyne

Typeset in Georgia 10 pt

IRON Press Books are distributed by Central Books
and represented by Inpress Books Ltd
Churchill House, 12 Mosley Street
Newcastle upon Tyne, NE1 1DE
Tel: 44(0) 191 2308104
www.inpressbooks.co.uk

Supported using public funding by
ARTS COUNCIL ENGLAND
LOTTERY FUNDED

DAVID ALMOND is the author of *Skellig, Kit's Wilderness, The Savage, The True Tale of the Monster Billy Dean, Mouse Bird Snake Wolf* and many other novels, stories and plays. His work is translated into over forty languages and is widely adapted for stage and screen.

His many awards include The Carnegie Medal, The Michael L Printz Award and The Hans Christian Andersen Award 2010, the world's most prestigious prize for children's authors.

David Almond is Professor of Creative Writing at Bath Spa University. He was born in Newcastle, grew up in Felling-on-Tyne and now lives in Northumberland. His first stories were published in IRON magazine and first two collections by IRON Press.

INTRODUCTION

THE FIRST STORY I EVER FINISHED PROPERLY WAS CALLED CHICKENS. I typed it up and sent it to Peter Mortimer at Iron Magazine. Three days later he wrote back saying that he loved it, that he wanted to publish it in the magazine. I still have that letter somewhere, I still have the sense of astonishment it brought. I'd been writing, through childhood, through university, through my first years of teaching. This was the first time I'd submitted anything to a proper magazine, to a proper editor. And look what had happened!

Years of writerly uncertainty followed, of course, the kind of uncertainty that never goes away. No surprise in that. Nobody comes along to you when you're young and says, 'You must be a writer my lad. You must send your deathless words into the world. Great acclaim, great joy and great wealth await!' You write because you're driven to write, because even at the worst of times, you love to write. You put away the thoughts of the millions of others just like you who are chasing the same editors and publishers. You stamp your feet and turn your nose up at rejection. You do the best work you can in the best way you can and you hope. And you write for the weird unmatchable joy of it; for the hard work and the routine; for the scribbling and doodling and pondering and wondering;

for the spontaneous workings of the imagination; for the moments when the words, characters, images begin to come to life on the page before you; for those strange moments of grace when the story does seem to be telling itself, when its voice seems to be speaking through you and discovering its own true form. And yes, you write for publication, for the moment when the story has left you, has become an independent thing and is on its own, out in the world, in the company of its readers.

I sent my stories to many little magazines, some of whose readers could be counted in tens. They were edited by poets, short story writers, rebels, enthusiasts. As well as in *IRON*, my work appeared over a couple of decades in *Argo, Kudos, Prospice, Not Poetry, Northern Electric News, Critical Quarterly, Sunk Island Review, Stand, The Echo Room, Raven, The Page, Edinburgh Review, The London Magazine, Panurge, Bananas* and others. It appeared in the fine Northern Stories anthologies published by Littlewood Press. A couple of stories were broadcast on BBC Radio 4. I gained a handful of keen readers. I became an editor myself, taking over *Panurge* from John Murray, and became one of those turning people away. Manuscripts clattered through the letterbox and thudded down into the hall. I received 1500 stories a year, and was able to publish 25 or so of them. Most of an editor's job, it became clear, was to say no.

I wrote that terrifying thing, a novel. I slogged away at it for five years. I sent it to every publisher in the land and every one of them said no. I spat, cursed, kept on, employing the thick skin, the doggedness, the degree of stupidity that every writer needs. I kept on writing stories, stories, more stories. And if there'd never be some kind of breakthrough, part of me simply didn't give a damn.

IRON published my stories consistently and enthusiastically. The magazine became a kind of home for me. IRON Press published my first collection, *Sleepless Nights*, in 1985. They published my second, *A Kind of Heaven*, in 1997. Most of the stories in *Nesting* are from those first two books. What a joy it was to see my stories gathered together then. What a pleasure it is to have them published by IRON Press again. As I wrote these stories, I had no idea that I'd one day become a children's writer. But life, and 'careers', are as unpredictable as decent fiction. I see that even back then I was exploring childhood, looking at the world through the eyes of the young, and I was beginning to draw strongly on the landscape and language of the north, beginning to allow forces from my own childhood to work upon my words. It seems to me I was more pessimistic back then, a little more dark than perhaps I am now. I've resisted the temptation to do a great deal of rewriting and polishing. I recognise myself. I see the roots of the writing I do now. It couldn't be otherwise, I guess. If we're driven to write, it's because there's something inside us that yearns to be written, to discover its form. It will have its way.

Telling stories is a very ordinary thing. We've been doing it since we gathered together in ancient caves. We'll be doing it until human time is done. Stories are all around us, in books, on TV, on radio, in cinema, on stage, in dance, in song, in bedtime tales, in gossip. We're imperfect beings in an imperfect world, and imperfection is at the heart of our complexity and creativity. Stories are where we come together, where we express ourselves and forget ourselves, where we are fiercely individual and profoundly social, where we work and play, where we approach profound unnameable truths in the attempt to create beautiful lies.

Writing can appear to be an individual act, but any individual needs a nurturing community. I, and these stories, were nurtured by a community of editors and their little magazines, particularly by Peter Mortimer and his heroic IRON Press. He has my lifelong thanks.

David Almond, March 2013

CONTENTS

13
JOFFY

28
A KIND OF HEAVEN

55
LUCY BLUE

62
FIRES

*

THE MARKET STORIES

93
CONCENTRIC RINGS

112
DARK CUBE

118
THE SNAKE CHARMER

121
THE EYE OF GOD

*

129
SPOTLIGHT

138
AFTER THE ABANDONED WHARVES

150
NESTING

164
1962

186
INSTEAD OF THE SCHEME

For Pete and Kitty

JOFFY

'Nn-nn-ooo-nnnooot... Nnnoott-en-enn...'

'Not enough? That's what you're saying, Joffy?'

'Yyyy-yy...'

The cleaver came down again, cutting away more from the red wedge of meat between the butcher's hands. Joffy, his head level with the marble slab, watched the pile of cubes before his eyes grow.

'How much more, Joffy? Your mammy only wrote steak.'

Joffy held the meat between his hands, then held his head in the same way.

'As big as your head,' his mother had said, sending him out. 'Get enough steak that would fill up your head.'

Faced with the meat now, though, he couldn't tell how much that was. It could be squashed, it fell into a sunken heap, but his head had its own hard shape. He looked up at the butcher, Mr McCaufrey, the only man who came to see them now, the only person, apart from those who came to pry and ask questions. Mr McCaufrey waited patiently, as usual, smiling, his face red as the blood on his broad hands, but this was too hard for Joffy. There was nowhere to begin. His tongue squirmed uselessly between his teeth.

'Tell you what, Joffy. You take this, and if you need more, you can come back for it. Okay?'

Walking the hill out of the village, Joffy could feel the meat sliding beneath the pressure of his fingers. He watched blood collect in the corners of the white plastic bag. He knew it didn't matter if there was too little or too much. She was angry anyway, and all yesterday, all this morning, had been shouting at him.

'The cow better not start nosing about again,' she said, her mouth twisted, scornful, 'She's just like the rest of us underneath it all. Thinks her money gives her some right, but it doesn't.'

The cow was Auntie Eileen. She was coming today, Saturday, to spoil it. On Saturdays he liked to be alone. His mother went out, not to return until the next morning, telling him he must stay near the house, go no further than the garden. He'd go to the quarry to sit by the pond there. It had begun to be packed with frogs now that spring was on its way. He'd play with them, until darkness came near, then run quickly home, trembling with anticipation.

But today he would have to stay with them, his mother and his aunt. Auntie Eileen had been before, and he hated her, was frightened by her. She wouldn't just leave him like most other people did, but was always wanting to touch him, fingering his skin, stroking his hair. Hardly anybody else did that. Hardly anybody else could. She always wanted to talk to him, kept asking him questions, telling him if he took his time he could say anything he wanted to. And she wore a fur hat and a fur scarf, even indoors. A fur scarf with animals' heads on its ends that hung down over her shoulders. She would pull him tightly to her huge soft chest, and he would have to stare into the animals' bright, empty eyes.

He approached his home, the last house in the village, a tiny bungalow isolated by high hawthorn hedges. Beyond it more hawthorn that edged the quarry, and link chain fences to keep the children out, because of falling stones. And far beyond the quarry the town where his school was, to which he travelled in what even his mother called the dooley bus. He hated entering the town in it, trying not to see the grinning bestial faces outside, put on to echo or provoke those inside.

Last time she was here, Auntie Eileen told his mother she should move from here, back into town, where there would be work for her, where Joffy could be close to school.

'We like it here, don't we, Joffy?" his mother said. 'We can keep ourselves to ourselves. It's fine, and there's plenty space for him.'

'Is it enough, though? There's hardly another child in the whole place. The boy needs friends, someone to be with, company.'

'Ha!'

Auntie Eileen turned to him, told him to say for himself that he would like friends, but he didn't know how to answer that. When she had gone, his mother, her fists full of five pound notes, muttered angrily all evening, more to the walls than to Joffy,

'Old bag, what does she know? Never had a cock in her whole life but tries to tell me what to do.'

Inside were the unfamiliar smells of disinfectant and polish. The living room was cleared of its piles of clothes, of its empty wine bottles. His mother was on the arm of a chair, still in her nightgown, putting on make-up before a small hand mirror. He held out the meat to her, but she waved it away in disgust, told him to leave it on the table. She smelt warm, newly bathed, and he went close to her, pressed himself to her. Sometimes she opened the gown, wrapped him inside it, but not today. With a long coloured fingernail she pushed him away from her, and as he left shouted after him,

'And mind you keep your trap shut today. You say nothing, not about anything. Right?'

She waited,

'Right?'

He turned, biting his lip, nodded.

White, tiny-headed, half-dumb Joffy. Into the hedge he went, to his damp dark nest of hollowed earth, broken branches, bark worn smooth by his so much sitting there. Joffy, white as a hawthorn petal, coloured only by sparse traceries of pink, pink eyes and his mouth when opened wide as red as any meat. He refused to look at himself now. He had long ago taught himself the horror of himself in mirrors, how he would peer out like some blanched fish used only to deep darkness. And fish-mouthed also, gulping silence.

Only on Saturday nights could he change. With her gone, he opened wide the door to her room, sat by her mirrors, spreading his face with her blacks, reds, greens, blues, made himself another Joffy that could glare out from the glass, run unrestrained and naked through the rooms, kicking walls, leaping from chair to chair, yelling his own invented words of savagery or hate. Then slept, in her bed, exhausted and smiling, travelling lucid jungles of colour and noise.

Sunday afternoons she returned, to the silent house, her made bed, Joffy peering at her, white and frightened from his nest.

'Joffy!'

She was calling him, standing in the doorway, in a skirt and a blouse buttoned to her throat, the remains of a cigarette dangling from her fingers.

'Out of there!'

Slapping his face as he came to her, calling him rat, yanking at his muddied trousers, pulling him in by his tangled hair.

'In here. Now. Look at you.'

She stripped him in the living room, cleaned him with licked tissues, dressed him in clothes bought yesterday, yellow jeans whose hems had to be turned up around his skinny ankles, shirt of pastel checks, running shoes, brushed his hair so fiercely close to his scalp he was certain the bristles came right through skin, scraped bone.

'Sit there. And dare move!'

He sat at the laid table's edge, gripping a knife blade so tightly his knuckles were white against his white, pressed to tears by his pain, her anger, his wildness that raced impotently beneath his skin and threw into his head pictures of animals' eyes, splashed frogs, carcasses hanging high behind opened white doors. But all that solved so easily when she came to him a half-hour later, sat him in her lap, tolerated his hands seeking her flesh beneath her blouse, his cheek pressed against her hair, whispered to him that he must be good this afternoon, good for her, and folded her arms about him, murmured,

'Little whiteness. My funny little whiteness.'

He was good, sat on the floor between them while they faced each other across the hearth. Auntie Eileen had seen his report from school. 'Jonathan likes art, and is good at it,' it said.

'Oh, Jonathan. Good boy,' she said, 'You must do some pictures for me.'

Crayons gripped in his fists he made furious tangles of colour for her, pressing so hard he gouged the edges of his paper to rags, spread flakes of wax across the floor. She wanted more, though, and she said,

'Oh, Jonathan, how lovely. You must tell me about it. I think I can see a dog there. And is this a house? Come and tell me.'

Waiting, without the animals' heads today, but her own head like a strange bird's, her eyes split by half-lens glasses, encouraging him, but Joffy unable to form answers for her, unable to think even of the beginnings of answers for her, his head seething with hatred for her. He simply nodded when she asked if what she saw there was there. He felt sick, the steak as big as his head, that she had cut into tiny pieces for him at lunch, resting like stones inside him, and he wanted only to be away from them, in the quarry, or lying asleep and coloured in his mother's bed.

When the women spoke with each other, it was as if they

believed that because he couldn't speak properly, he couldn't hear properly either. At the table it had been all the old things, how they should move from here, go back to town, stop being so cut off, how being here wasn't enough for the boy and was too much for his mother. His mother kept saying they managed, they liked it, it had been hell before they came here and was so much better now.

'But what future is there here?' Auntie Eileen said, 'How can the boy improve? How can you get pulled together again? Look at you. You're not the girl you were. Look at that poor lonely boy. You're just eating each other up.'

Until his mother could stand it no longer, angrily began to clear the table of dishes and unfinished meat, shouted,

'It's my life, my home, my boy. Fucking leave it like that!'

Joffy had only vague recollections of hell. Of standing spread-eagled on windowsills gazing far down to roaring city streets, of gripping his mother's loose hands in rattling lift shafts, echoing stairwells. He remembered the ache of her long absences, when he was shut alone behind his locked door with the huge distances below, his dreams of falling and his mother's howls, waking next day to find unknown hollow-eyed men repelled by his presence in his mother's arms. Hell had diminished now, was at a distance, in his journeys to school, her anger, the questioning of strangers. Nearer at hand were the comforts of his nest, the damp quarry, his mother's regular presence, the opportunity of pressing himself against her skin, his dense dreams. He wanted to stay here.

'You could find yourself a little job,' said Auntie Eileen, 'Nothing special, but something to hold body and soul

together. And there are so many nice flats now. We'd all help,
Elisabeth. It needn't be like it was.'

'How do you know how it was?'

'All that's past now, Elisabeth. It's different now. All we
want is the best for you. And for Jonathan.'

'And for you, for your guilt. Christ when I think of you all
then. You didn't give a shit what might happen.'

'Oh Elisabeth, can't we let what's past be past? Can't you
stop resisting? You could change your whole life, make it so
much better for you both. You could meet someone, someone
to share your lives with, but what chance have you of that
here?'

'Meet someone? A fine catch we'd make. A worn-out
twenty-five-year-old whore and her idiot child. Sure, they'd
be falling over themselves to get us.'

'Oh, Elisabeth.'

'It's true. Look at us. You said it.'

'Right from the start we said how it might turn out, but
you were so reckless, so determined to go on with it. As soon
as you decided you wanted the child you took the chance of
all this happening. But now that it has happened you can't
just ignore all your responsibilities, you can't just hide and
hope they'll go away.'

'You're all the same. You, social workers, those buggers
at the school. How am I treating him, am I doing right, is this
the way to live? Everything about him, worrying about him.
How do you know what it's like, having him here all the time,
something that came out of you and you can't get rid of.'

'He's your child, Elisabeth. The child you wanted.'

'Yes, I wanted the child, but I didn't want him.'

'You don't mean that.'

'Don't I? Sometimes I want to hurt him so much that you won't be able to leave him with me, but you'll have to take him away from me, and leave me alone, let me be myself again, and not just the idiot who got knocked up with her first fuck.'

They were silent then. His mother pressed her face to her fists. Auntie Eileen leaned forward, laid her palm on his skull. Joffy searched his dreams that even in daytime could be more real than his diminished hell, and found one. Sitting surrounded by failing light and his name repeated over and over, he dashed through the tangles of himself to a shallow pond at his centre. He found frogs there, lifted them from the water, packed them in white plastic, dashed them against rocks. In his head and on his paper red mingled fiercely with green, until he exhausted himself, and slept, on swampy ground, feeling water seep through his thin new clothes, dreaming a deeper Joffy, a fleshy mud-burrowing creature, a worm, an eel, a dark Joffy sucking the dark.

'Joffy.'

His mother's voice, calmer now, soothing, extracting him from sleep.

'Sleepyhead, come on.'

Darkness, the windows dark pink patches of sky and black tips of hedges. Her hands under his armpits and her mouth pressed close to him, whispering. Auntie Eileen standing there, her smile cracked even in the dark. Lifted up to find his mother with his coat, manipulating him into it, saying he would be fine, fine. Lifted again, higher, into Auntie Eileen's arms, pressed to her chest, and she laughed, saying how small he was, how frail. She carried him out into the dusk, his mother opening the door and the garden gate for them, then leaning down to unlock the car door, opening that. Together they lowered him through it, began fastening a belt about his chest, fumbling with the buckle at his waist.

'Mammy!'

After the surprised pause, his mother soothing him again.

'Joffy don't worry it'll be all right. You're going away for a few days to Auntie Eileen's, that's all. Then I'll come for you and never again leave you. We'll go together to somewhere new and never come here again, and everything will be better again, better than it's ever been. Joffy are you listening? Do you understand? Soon everything will be fine. Oh, Joffy it'll be heaven. Be good for me, be good.'

'Every day I'll take you somewhere in the car,' said Auntie Eileen. 'You just choose somewhere, Jonathan, and we'll go there. What do you say to that? Won't it be wonderful?'

Joffy said nothing, knew only that he would not go. He pulled away the belt, squirmed from their grip, ran back into the house and did not stop running until he had stooped through his nest, scrambled through hedges, pulled himself over the link chain fence, skidded on his backside over the rubble and waste at the quarry's edge, struggled through the bracken and bramble on the quarry's floor, and come finally to the pond, a thin slick of water from which the exposed stone rose in a vertical wall. Then he rested, crouched in the undergrowth, licking his torn skin, tasting his blood. No noise but his breathing, his rapid heartbeat, far-off traffic, small animals scratching the weeds. Nothing to see but the water's glistening, branches and the quarry's rim against the sky, a few pale stars, and his hands when he lifted them, their white bloom.

For minutes, nothing but that. Then they came, only their voices at first, calling him from the direction of the house, until he saw their black outlines above him, one on each side of him, travelling the quarry's edge, until over his head they met, by now his mother furious.

'Joffy you're in there! Get out of it! Come on, out!'

She threatened him, that she would flay his hide, that the police would come, that someone would come to take him away for ever from her. He moved only to settle himself closer to the earth, to lift his coat over his head. In the blackness he tried to remove himself from his hearing, from her noise

'The rats'll get you. The snakes'll crawl all over you. There's a man in those bushes waiting to strangle you.'

It was all he found, a night in himself echoing with her words.

'Right. Stay there. Stay all night. Stay forever. I'm well rid of you. Don't ever come back!'

The voices stopped. Footsteps left him.

Never before except in dreams had he been here at night. He went to the stone and stood with his back to it, staring out of himself, holding rocks in his hands, ready to fling them at any of the horrors predicted by his mother. He felt exposed, white skin glowing in the quarry's black, so smothered his hands in mud, spread his face with it. Dead still again, too scared to blink even, he stood, while the moon lifted itself into the sky, picked out black incomprehensible shadows from the black. Anything could be seen now, any arrangement of hooves, horns and tails, the glint of eyes staring back at him, heads high and misshapen as piled stones, impossible birds ready to fall from shrubs. He wanted to disappear, to be anything but the focus of all this, to be plant, water, soil, stone, anything but Joffy, but it was an age that he stood there being Joffy, Joffy, Joffy.

'Joffy!'

A man's voice, from the quarry's entrance, reassuring him, searching him out.

'Joffy where are you lad? Make a noise and I'll come for you. Don't worry, everything's fine. Come on, Joffy, make a noise.'

Joffy crawled towards the voice, saw the man outlined between fence posts against the sky, behind him the still figures of the two women.

'Joffy it's me, Mr McCaufrey. Come on, I'll help you out.'

The butcher stepped down, onto the waste, became a hardly distinguishable descending shadow, florid face lost among so much dark. On the quarry floor, he was noise, the snapping of twigs and stems, a gross blundering body calling, 'Joffy, Joffy, Joffy.' And Joffy grinned, knowing himself dominant, knowing this place, knowing himself small, mud-covered, silent. It was easy to roll unnoticed from the butcher's clumsiness. Easy to go on grinning, snigger when the butcher finally called to the women that it was hopeless, that he could see nothing, that maybe the boy wasn't there anyway, and began to make his way out of the quarry towards them. And when he was once more visible against the sky, it was easy for Joffy to allow his sniggering to rise in pitch and loudness, to become a wild piercing noise ringing from the dark to the adults high above.

When he had calmed, they were gone, leaving him to stay, he supposed, as his mother had said, forever. He stood up, picked his way over the waste, climbed the fence, stood watching. Through the hedges shone the village lights, nearest to him those of his home. He went towards them, came to his nest, saw from there the adults inside talking, shaking their heads. He stood at the window, heard his mother sure he would return. They should go, she said, or he'd stay out there all night. She would call for the butcher if he were needed. Auntie Eileen should come back another day, when they'd try again. The butcher and Auntie Eileen left. Over the rooftops Joffy heard the car starting, the butcher's heels on the pavement, subdued farewells. Joffy laughed, and remained standing there, knowing he would not be seen, when his mother came to stare out between her hands into the night. When she came out, he pressed himself close to the wall, allowed her to pass within inches of him. She crouched at his nest, pulled branches and weeds aside, cursed him.

Grinning, he went into the house, stood by the fireside, waiting.

She said nothing. Everything seemed long prepared for. Hardly looking at him, she took his arm, led him to the bathroom where she undressed and bathed him, dried him with coarse towels that left his skin stinging. He showed no sign of complaint. Nothing seemed required of him. She took him to his room, pulled aside the covers on his bed, laid him face down on it.

'I'll tame you, boy,' she said, her voice now drained of anger and scorn.

She took a belt from her waist, pinned his neck to the bed with her free hand, and beat him until he could be silent no longer. He screamed, tried to thrash away from the pain, but there was no release until he abandoned himself to it, allowed it to fall into him, covering him over, leaving him finally insensitive in a dark silence where there was nothing, no Joffy at all.

Hours of dreamless sleep had passed when he opened his eyes, found himself standing outside his tangled bed. He walked like Joffy always wanted to walk, erect, his head high.

Outside her window, stars, as far away as pain, clustered thickly about the moon's ring. From her mirror's rim, light shone on him, on his white face, white as petals, paper, snow, as everything that had ever been white. White as the absence of all dark, of any hint of shade. He changed it: with her lipsticks, creams and powders made another Joffy's face, striped, spotted, starred, a rain of glistening dust falling across its surface. And mascaraed his hair into a stiff mane, black as night.

He stood over her, waiting, but there was only her breathing, her eyes flickering violently beneath their lids.

'Mammy,' he said, 'Mammy.'

Even before she was fully awake, she was smiling at him,

gazing far into him, and he felt himself being filled with her, so that there was no room for anything but her.

'Mammy, let me in.'

She lifted the bedclothes, drew him towards her, held him close to her.

'Mammy, let me stay,' he said, and all night, as if forever, his peculiarly coloured features roamed her white skin.

A KIND OF HEAVEN

Why had he been so scared? She seemed well, that morning they left the house above the beach, headed to the city, the day he encountered Harris for the first time.

Icy and bright. The sun rising. Threads of frost in the ribbed sand. The sea like burnished metal, an almost imperceptible swell.

She burst in on him, dragged him from his bed, held him at the window.

'Such a day,' she said. 'Look at the glow in it. Look at the shine from it. And you in bed. You and him both in bed.'

As he dressed, through the open doors he heard her counting coins into her purse, heard her laughing with his father. 'Stuffy thing,' she called him. 'Old misery.' He heard them struggling together on the bed, their exclamations of effort and pain, their joy, her cry,

'Tom, rescue me! Tom, come and rescue me.'

The father, in his dressing gown, chased them from the house and they ran out hand in hand onto the road above the beach. They halted there, stood pulling on their coats and scarves.

'Old misery!' she called. 'We're well rid of you, old man!'

From the gate he shook his fist at her.

'Of you and all!' he yelled. 'Of you and him and all!'

They took the bus to Newcastle, headed down towards the quay.

The city was silent, but for the footsteps of the others going down with them, their raised voices and laughter. She was in scarlet, the skirt of her coat swinging against him with every step. He kept watching her, checking her, then turning to the others, waiting for them to be drawn by her. They were on Dean Street, steep curve of massive buildings, Victorian and black, leading to the river shining from below. Above their heads, the platform of the bridge headed out dead straight between the roofs, the arch stretched into the sky.

Sunday. Market day. Rows of stalls between the warehouses; narrow, white-canopied alleyways filled with the smell of meat frying, the voices of crowds and stallholders, music pouring from transistors – tunes left over from the war, skiffle and Presley, the Beatles' wail. She held a shirt against him, mused, shook her head. She lifted dresses and hats towards herself, posed for him. 'This?' she asked. 'Or this one? Does it do anything for me?' She laid it all back on the stalls – 'Tat,' she called it. 'Nothing but tat.' – and bought only a singlet for her husband, with, 'Poor soul. Needs the warmth these days. Needs a bit of caring.' Outside the alleyways, they stood at the water's edge. She smeared mustard onto hot beef sandwiches and they stood pressed close together by the passing crowd, laughing at the unwieldiness of the food, catching the juices with their tongues. And they groaned with pleasure, cleaned each other with her handkerchief, kissed each other.

Outside the canopies, a crowd had gathered at the foot of

a crane. She pulled him to it, stood on tiptoe, peered through.

'No!' she gasped. 'Never! No!'

'What is it?' he demanded, straining to see, failing. 'What's happening?'

She laughed at his confusion.

'In there, look. In the middle, Tom.'

'I see nothing.'

'It's Harris. Little Harris has returned.'

And she took his hand, led him through towards the centre.

Harris was short, squat, naked to the waist. There were blurred tattoos on his skin, dozens of little nicks and bruises. He had a small sack hooked to the tip of a cane. He thrust it out at the spectators, glared at them.

'Get your money out,' he told them. 'There's nothing to be seen till you pay.'

Behind him, a cartwheel rested against the crane. There was a knapsack, a heap of chains and locks, a blanket opened out to reveal a range of needles and pins and skewers.

Tom looked at her, nudged her.

'Watch,' she said. 'Just watch and wait.'

Harris saw them, newcomers, thrust his sack at them.

'Get your money out,' he said. 'There's nothing to see till you pay.'

As she dropped in her pennies he glared at Tom, fixed him with his stare.

'For him and all,' he said. 'The squirt there. Make sure you've paid for him and all.'

They waited. Time after time he thrust the sack into the

crowd. He kept pulling it back, counting the coins in there, peering back at the spectators with disappointed eyes, telling them, 'Not for this, oh no. Risk so much for this?' And he'd come at them again, each time louder in his demands, each time more pugnacious, and Tom in his frustration kept asking her,

'How long? How long's he going to take?'

'An age,' she told him. 'Always an age. Some days we'd stand an hour or more and see nothing but his yelling and stamping his feet. Good to see him. I thought he'd moved on, died even. Harris. Little Harris. After all these years.'

Behind them the crowd had increased. They were being shuffled forward, the space around Harris was diminishing. He leaned into the crowd, stretched his arm out across their shoulders, demanded payment from the back. From somewhere catcalls and whistling had started.

'Impatient, eh?' he shouted. 'Want the show started, eh? Then get your cash out. Pay your way. Nothing's for nothing.'

And Tom sighed.

'Do something,' he whispered, gripping his mother's hand tight. 'Drop the sack and do something.'

Harris at last recoiled from his audience. He held up a few coins, as if he were in despair. He laid the cane and sack on the ground. He lifted the cartwheel onto its rim, rolled it until it was upright in front of him. He lifted it, a few inches, let it drop to the ground and Tom felt the concrete shuddering beneath his feet.

'Best timber,' said Harris. 'Best steel. Listen.' And he lifted it again, dropped it again. 'Some body in it, eh?'

He stood watching, taking deep breaths, blowing out air, sucking it in. The watchers were still being pressed forward by those at the back. He cried out as he lifted the wheel, and it stilled them all. He lifted it in one movement, leaned his head back, rested the rim on his brow. He stamped, settling himself, then took his hands from the wheel and left it resting there. He took little steps, he held his arms out wide, kept adjusting himself as the wheel threatened to fall. The muscles in his neck stretched and bulged, his cries were strangled in his throat. The crowd edged back now, scared that the wheel would fall. Someone was giggling, others were yelling, urging him on. His mother held Tom tight. She was smiling. 'Nothing changes,' she said. 'Still the same.' Soon Harris reached up to the wheel again, lifted it free, rested it in front of him. Released from the weight, he jumped several times, then stared out. There were tears in his eyes, little pieces of dirt and grit were embedded in his brow.

'Poor Harris,' she whispered. 'Poor soul.'

'The wheel,' he said. 'The wheel. What's next? Who wants to chain Harris? Who wants to lock the chains round his throat and his limbs and say, there Harris, no getting out of that? Eh? Eh? Or the needles. The pins and needles sticking out?' He came at the crowd, glaring, thrusting his face at them. 'Get your loot out. Get your money out and pay.' He lifted the cane and the sack. 'Give,' he demanded. 'Get giving.' He muscled his way into the crowd. 'You,' he said. 'And you. You haven't paid. You haven't. And you and all.'

The crowd began to disperse. Many of those at the front turned back towards the stalls, letting those at the back come through. Tom was being drawn away by his mother. 'He'll make us wait an age for this,' she said. He followed her towards the water's edge. They headed for the bridge. From behind came Harris' calling. 'Where you going? Why you leaving? You and all. Always something else to see.' Tom turned, saw Harris standing outside the crowd now. Harris caught his eye, beckoned to him. 'Squirt!' he yelled. 'And you! That pretty one! Where you off to? Why?'

She pulled Tom on. She was laughing. 'Don't look back,' she said. 'Or he'll never let you get away.' The river ran a dozen feet below them. There were gulls screaming, riding the gentle breezes at the river's centre.

'Harris,' she said. 'Fancy. Little Harris. Your father should have come.'

'Who is he?'

'He was in Egypt with your father. Came back with him, on the same boat home. Poor soul. He'd had too much. The war, the heat. They'd got to him.'

In the shade beneath the bridge, they caught their breath. The air was bitter, frost remained. They waited at the foot of the bridge's stone column, waiting for the lift to come. She drew him into the shelter formed by the massive curves of steel descending to meet the quay. Leaning back, feeling the huge rivets of the bridge pressing on his spine, he watched her shudder, watched her fasten tight the scarlet collar at her throat.

'Damned place,' she said, and the laughter had left her eyes, her voice was trembling. 'So bitter cold. Keeps on telling me he'll take us off to the pyramids for a winter, make us miss all this. Cairo. Do you believe it?'

The lift came. A little man on a stool inside the door escorted them. Tom saw how the man watched her, how he couldn't take his eyes off her.

'Madam,' the man said after the ascent, holding back the steel gates for her. 'And young sir as well.' She dropped a coin into a box on the wall. 'So kind. Thank you, madam.'

She giggled, stepping out, gasped at the wind that was blowing freely here. She started running, took Tom's hand and dashed towards the centre of the bridge. She leaned over the parapet, he peered through its rails, saw her face filling the sky, hair streaming in the wind. She leaned further, further, till her head was inverted, almost level with his own, and she laughed, 'Hold me, Tom! Keep me back!' And in terror he swivelled and clutched her, both arms around the knees.

'Silly thing,' she said. 'Silly thing. I couldn't fall.'

She crouched by him, held her arm across the parapet, showed him the warehouses packing the wharves, the tangle of cranes stretching east towards the sea. Half a mile away a white liner was docked.

'Maybe that'd take us,' she said. 'Maybe that'd get us somewhere away from this.'

Her hair swept across his throat. The wind whipped away her scent, her breath. Her voice mingled with the screaming of the gulls. He lowered his head, stared through the gaps towards the quay: neat arrangement of white canopies and stalls, slowly moving crowd. Beneath the crane he saw the tight circle of spectators with Harris at their centre. He was a tiny tortured figure, jerking and squirming on the ground.

'Look,' he said.

'The chains,' she said. 'The locks and chains.'

And he wanted to ask her more, but suddenly she was away, and he couldn't catch her, and she was yelling,

'Race you to the other side!' They held each other tight, returning. The platform of the bridge led them straight towards the city's heart. All around, on road and pavement and the bridge's steel, frost was forming, sparkling in the brilliant late light. When he raised his head, he was astonished to see a pale moon already hanging over the roofs and spires and stacks.

'But of course,' she chided. 'Short days, Tom. Winter. Early nights.'

And as they left the bridge, entered the city's streets, the sky began to change, streaks of colour began to gather in the west. They spread and deepened, made the emptiness above them bleed and flame.

'What will become of us?' she sighed, stopping at a newspaper seller's stall, looking down at Khrushchev with his fists raised, at headlines demanding that the bomb tests must go on, we must always be prepared, we mustn't hesitate. 'No time since men were exhausted or made mad by it all, since they came back telling us never, never again.'

The newspaper seller held out his cupped palm, muttered curses, then yelled after them as they moved away.

'No good running off! It's coming soon! It'll catch you soon!'

'Yes, it's coming,' she whispered, and the boy had to strain to hear her. 'It'll come again.'

In the dimly lit station, waiting at their bay, they leaned towards each other, stamped their feet, kept exclaiming at the cold, kept laughing, breaking into little jigs.

'This'll be it,' they cried at each new set of headlights appearing in the streets outside. 'No, the next one... the next but one.'

Outside, on the monument, the angel stood as always, poised for flight above the heap of fighting men.

'When I count to thirty,' she said. 'One, two...'

'No, ten!'

And he rushed into his counting, till eight, when he left a massive gulf till nine, then started out again with,

'Nine and one millionth... nine and two millionths...'

'Fool!' she said, and she cuffed him, the woollen-gloved hand falling gently across his cheek. 'Millionths!'

The fire in the sky faded, the moon became bright. He pointed out the stars he'd learned from his father on the pitch black beach.

'The Archer,' he said. He traced it, followed its pattern with his outstretched arm. She crouched, her head level with his, allowing him to show her.

'His belt, you see. His bow, his arm drawn back. The arrow's tip.'

'Oh, yes,' she said. 'I think I see.'

He laughed. 'You don't,' he said. 'Not that quick. Course you don't.' He nudged her, and she grinned at him. 'It's hard,' he said. 'But once you see, it's easy. You'll see him standing there night after night after night.'

'It's all made up, of course,' he said, when they were

standing, jigging again. 'His stars have got nothing to do with each other. It's just the way they look to us, from where we are in everything.'

The bus arrived at last. They sat huddled on the long back seat.

'He'll think we've run away,' she said, and she giggled. 'He'll think we've found a handsome rich devil to take us away from this.'

'He'll think we've been kidnapped. He'll think they've got us in a dark cellar somewhere and want a fortune to give us back.'

'He'll think: Thank God – I'm rid of those two brats.'

'They're off my back at last.'

'He's in for a shock, then, eh?'

The bus rattled out from the city. He kept turning to her, stealing glances. It made her laugh. 'Who d'you think you're looking at?' she asked, turning to the window, haughty. She was well, so well. In the blackness beyond the streetlights the boy slept against her. In his dream, Harris crouched half-naked in the frost beneath the bridge. He was wrapped in chains, padlocked, the nicks on his body were fresh wounds trickling with blood. Behind him, far beyond the river and the city's fringes, the horizon was aflame: real fire raging to the sky. 'Squirt,' he whispered. 'You. Squirt.' He sneered at the boy's mother, fixed the boy with his eye. 'Her an all,' he whispered. 'The red-coated one, that pretty one, her an all.'

He woke to her talking of food, what would be waiting for them.

'...hot stew with little crisp dumplings. The house filled

with the smell of it, everywhere heated by the oven and the fire all day long. Carrots cut longways with that buttery coating of his, spinach bright green and oh so tender to cut. Can you imagine it, Tom? Can you taste it?'

He buried his face in her coat, let her words move Harris from his mind.

'…warm honey seeping from the warm cake, mingling with the white sauce… licking your lips to catch every last drop of it, holding it on your tongue a moment more, a moment more…'

In their village they descended from the bus to find his father rushing out of the darkness at them.

'Where've you been?' he demanded. 'Where've you bloody been?'

And they hurried home, laughing at the unevenness of the lane above the beach, gripping each other tight each time another stumbled. She kept talking of Harris, little Harris, poor Harris.

'Poor Harris!' said her husband. 'He's a wild man. Should've stayed out with the snake charmers and the dervishes. Had his brains boiled – too much sun, too many magic men…'

Inside, the rooms were as warm as she'd anticipated. They ate small pasties hot from the oven, with carrots as she'd said and potatoes whipped into a cream. Afterwards there was rice, creamy and sweet beneath its scorched skin.

Much later, Tom opened his eyes, looked out from his bed to see the Archer poised above the sea. He heard waves slapping at the rocks, and as he fell asleep again, heard his parents murmuring their pleasure in the night...

'Trickery, nothing more. War brought them out. Charlatans from Cairo's cellars. Brought them heading up from the desert with their antics and their potions and their hands held out. A higher form of begging, nothing more. They'd squat there in the squares stroking cobras. They'd have swords rammed down their throats, nails in their nostrils. They'd chain themselves into bags and boxes and nets and they'd lie sunk for minutes at a time in tanks of filthy water. Sorcery? They were wild men, crazed men. Who knows what they took that bubbled through their blood? They wouldn't sit in the corners patient and abject like the others, with their deliberately severed limbs and their eyes burned out. They had to perform, had to confront you, had to pursue you if you turned away. You, mister! You pay, mister! Glaring at you, eyes wild, brains boiled, scuffling down the alleys after you. Pay, mister! You pay!'

They were on the beach, on the firm sand left by the ebbing tide. Fishing boats, surrounded by gulls, headed in from the horizon. They walked slowly north, towards the headland, past coal gatherers knee-deep in the water with their sieves, separating black fragments of coal from the beige sand. At the water's edge stood the ponies and carts, the stuffed sacks. The beach narrowed, became a thin strip bounded by water on one side, tank traps left from the war on the other. Another bright day, the sun on its low trajectory through an unblemished sky.

Tom kept turning to his father, wanting the silence to be broken again.

'Harris believed it all, you see. He told us these people had conquered something in themselves. He said they felt no pain, that they had no desires. He believed that their contortions and their scars were signs that they had disciplined themselves, that they had risen above the world. He was there too long. The heat, the war. He fell for it, for all of it. Your mother's right. Poor Harris. Poor bloody Harris. What was the pain he wanted to blot out? I remember on the boat, all of us sitting round him, the first time I saw him with the needles, running them through the lighter flame then sticking them in all over himself. At each needle he shuts his eyes a moment, a little gasp, opens them again with a light shining there like he's proud, so proud, like he's knowing something none of the audience'll ever know. And all the time the guys giggling and nudging each other and going, That's right, Harris, get the buggers in, until he starts whispering and we all close down and hear him going, Nothing, nothing, nothing. And in the end he gets this skewer, one of them we've eaten lumps of meat off and he starts shoving it in through his cheek right where the jawbone is and pushing further with the blood trickling so we can hardly bear to go on watching. And those that do watch see the skewer coming out the other cheek, pressing the skin out to a point until it bursts through and the blood's running down his other cheek now and the point's coming further out, and his eyes are tight shut, tight shut, till finally he opens them again and he's looking out at us but like he sees none of us, and some of us get close and stare deep and see the skewer right across the entrance to his throat, and all the time he's sighing, sighing, sighing. Just like the sighs a man makes when he loves... Harris. Once the boat docked, thought I'd seen the last of him. Till down on the quay one Sunday with your mother and she says, What's going on here? And I look through the crowd and there he is, yelling, Pay! Get your bloody money out! It's Harris, I say, It's bloody Harris. And I push through to him, wondering will he know me, and I stand right in front of him but all he does is jab me with his money bag, and tell me, For her an all, that pretty one, for her an all, and sees nothing in me, remembers nothing of me. Harris. I'll have to see him. Thought he'd've moved on by now. Thought he'd be dead by now...'

At the headland they squatted on the rocks. The water sucked and spat, draining through ancient channels, leaving the pools, brilliant pools filled with the deep blueness of sky, that held within themselves bright weeds and mosses, unfolding anemones. They lifted rocks, laughed at the crabs scuttling back into cover, the tiny fish that dashed into the weed. Once Tom plunged his hand deep into a pool, took out a crab, held it between thumb and forefinger, while the legs waved and the claws snapped uselessly. He placed his fingertip inside a claw, let it grip him, and he giggled: it was just a tickling, that was all.

They turned back, headed home. Small gusts of wind swept dry sand inches-high across the wet sand. It tingled at their ankles. Inland, they saw frost in the depressions in the dunes, and twenty miles away snow lay covering the Cheviots. His mother was out, tiny green-clothed figure waving from the gate and calling them. Tom waved back, leaping high and swinging his arms above his head.

Closer to home, his father asked quietly,

'How was she, on Sunday in town?'

Tom stared.

'Energetic? Able to take a day of it?'

Tom nodded.

'Course she was,' he said. 'You should have seen her, running full pelt on the bridge.'

There'd be places with little pain. He'd been told that. At school they'd drawn maps of their hands. Tom had closed his eyes while his friend Askew touched the skin with the needle's point. 'Where am I touching now?' said Askew. 'What can you feel now?' And it was true. There were places almost without sensation, where Askew could press harder, and Tom would hear the smile in his voice as he asked, 'Nothing, eh? And here? And now?' Together they mapped the points of pain and the points of nothingness, and then Tom sat gazing down at the pinpricks on his skin while the teacher asked, 'So what have we learned from this? What conclusions can be drawn? Why are some parts of us more sensitive than other parts...?'

He repeated the exercise now, in the solitude of his room. It was dusk, the Archer was forming, he heard the sea sliding across the sand, coming in. He sat at the bed's edge, bare-chested, closing his eyes each time he touched his body with the point. Where was he touching now? And now? He tried to separate himself from the knowledge of what his hand and arm were doing. This was impossible. He knew he was both donor and receiver of the pain. But still there were moments when he doubted this, when he had to open his eyes and see that the needle was indeed being pressed into his skin; and moments when his hand recoiled and he gasped at the intensity of what had been intended as a gentle touch.

He pulled on his shirt, dropped the needle when he heard them coming up. He listened. How slow was she? What help did she need? She'd slept most of the evening downstairs, after complaining of the cold, the damned cold. Tom had stared at his father. It was nothing, he'd been told. Nothing. They watched TV together in silence. Every half hour there came news of war, the cold war. Again and again they saw Khrushchev storming out, saying it couldn't go on, the treaties must end. Once they caught each other's eye, half in panic, when she suddenly gasped in her sleep, drew her knees to her chest, but when she woke at last she'd been dreaming of Derwent Water, of waking early, looking out across the still water towards Catbells and Skiddaw. The honeymoon, the story Tom knew so well: bus journey through the Pennines to the Lakes; the Lodore; how had they been able to afford it? Walking out as if into their kingdom; the fells and water; the rocky summits; sunlight; joy; world's rebirth. He listened again as they drew from their memories images that were so familiar to him that they might almost have been authentic memories of his own, were it not for the fact that only two of them existed then, only two of them walked hand in hand there, only two of them were reunited, released at last from war. And for the first time Tom understood his isolation, his exclusion from them. The heaven they described was theirs, and could exist only in memory, in the years between the war's end and his birth.

'Tom?' she'd said, reaching out to him. 'Tom?'

He sat stiffly, feeling her eyes on him.

'What is it, Tom?'

He shrugged. His eyes were burning. He motioned to the TV.

'Why do they call it that?' he asked. 'Why do they say the war is cold?'

They hadn't been able to answer him. He'd kissed them, come upstairs.

He listened. They whispered, they sighed. He heard what sounded like her sudden cry of pain. There was a knock at his door, his father entered.

'Still sitting up, I see.'

'The stars. Just watching.'

'Ah. No windows open, have you?'

'No.'

'We'll close the curtains, though. So cold. Draughts everywhere.'

Leaving, he hesitated at the door.

'Probably come to nothing, you know. We've had it before, all this threatening, sabre-rattling. What we'll do and what we won't do to each other. My bomb's bigger than your bomb. It's a game, son, just a bloody game.'

'Probably.'

'It's sick. But we'll survive.' He leaned down, touched the boy's shoulder. 'Whatever happens, we'll survive. Yes?'

Tom looked up, but his tongue was stilled by unaskable,

unanswerable questions.

'Yes,' said his father. 'Yes. Yes, yes, yes.'

Afterwards, when there was only the sound of their regular breathing and the waves were washing the sand, Tom dropped from his bed to crawl on hands and knees, seeking the needle, but it was nowhere. When he slept, he felt the massive rivets of the bridge pressing on his spine. They were bending him, forming him. Where was she? He scanned the quays. He stretched high, but all was silent, deserted. The river was metallic, the sun glared from the middle of the sky. He kept on growing, he arched, stretched from quay to quay with the river far below him. Then he saw her, tiny, scarlet-coated. She stood at the parapet, smiling, then ran, turned, ran again. She ran full pelt with her coat tails flying, running and turning, held within him, safe.

He went again, this time with his father. She saw their reluctance to leave her, but she scorned their fears. 'Get going,' she said. 'I'm well rid of you.' Her turn to cook, she said. She'd have it waiting for their return. She arranged them both, tugging their collars closer to their throats. 'Can't have my men cold. Can't have them going out uncared-for.' She giggled. 'And watch him, Tom. Don't let Harris hex him, get him running off to sunny Cairo and leaving us alone.'

There'd been sun, but all morning clouds had been heading from the Cheviots. Now sleet was falling, making thick splashes on the window of the bus.

His father wore brown herringbone coat, brown trilby, brown brogues. Tom kept wiping away the condensation, staring out, watching it form again.

As they entered the city, his father laughed suddenly.

'And skins, all that stuff about skins! He said he'd seen men who'd dress in the skin of a beast and become the beast. Men in leopard skins snarling like leopards. Men wearing antelope skin and leaping high as antelopes. Lion skin, ape skin, snake skin. He reeled them off. Ship's fool. You either ignored him or humoured him. Except the ones that got enough of him, and did their damage in the dark below decks. I found him myself one morning in a heap on the stairs with his clothes all ripped and his skull cracked open. What's happened, I asked him. What've the buggers done? Nothing, he said. Nothing. Harris. Poor sod.'

The sleet gathered as slush in doorways and on windowsills. It melted, ran down the gutters towards the quay. The streets were almost deserted, a few people heading down, stooped forward, protecting themselves with umbrellas, wide-brimmed hats, collars tugged tight.

'Can't see him coming out in this,' said his father. 'We should have stayed. Shouldn't have come.'

Tom kept looking up, over the rooftops but the bridge stretched into low-lying clouds, its summit was lost in them. The river was dark grey, agitated by wind and a turning tide. Among the stalls, water dripped from the canopies, the stallholders stared gloomily out.

They ate hot beef sandwiches, and Tom said,

'It's good she didn't come. She'd have hated this.'

'Aye. It'd do her no good.'

A tinny transistor was playing dance music: a big band,

sounding so dated now.

They roamed the alleyways, but found nothing. They half-heartedly inspected the tacky goods for sale. Tom passed over a few coins to buy a brilliant blue scarf for his mother. It was a loosely woven, inadequate thing, but they praised its colour, said it might be useful when the weather broke. The only place that held them more than a few seconds was the joke stall, where they laughed together at the fake boils and warts, the monkey masks, the turds, the nails that could appear to pierce fingers, the packets of powders and bottles of smells.

Outside, the clouds didn't lift. Beyond the sound of dripping water and music, foghorns wailed from the direction of the sea.

It was useless. He wouldn't come. 'Let's go back,' said Tom. Relieved, they left the canopies. They were heading back to Dean Street when Tom turned towards the bridge and saw Harris sheltering there. He sat on an upturned crate, the cartwheel was resting at his side, he had a knapsack laid on the ground beside him. Tom took his father's hand, led him there, and Harris kept his face turned towards the earth as they approached. Out of the sleet, beneath the bridge, they relaxed, stood ten yards from Harris.

He wore an ancient and sodden blue striped suit, torn collarless shirt. He had a tweed cap pulled tight over his head. He had a cigarette cupped in his hand, kept drawing on it.

Tom heard his father whispering, 'Jesus. Jesus Christ.'

Harris tilted his head, was staring back at them. He spat, then held out his hand towards them. Tom felt in his pockets.

A few pennies. He went to Harris, dropped them into his palm. He smelt the alcohol on Harris' breath, saw the scorn in his eyes when he looked down at Tom's offering.

'For this?' he grunted. 'For this?'

Tom was backing off but Harris caught him, grabbed his sleeve.

'Him and all,' he said. 'That bugger there.'

Tom's father came forward. He dropped coins of his own into Harris' palm. He stood over him.

'Harris,' he said.

Harris stared back at him, empty.

'Do you know me, Harris? Remember me?'

Harris rattled the coins, listening, as if he were enchanted by their ringing.

'We were in Egypt, Harris. We came home on the same boat. You were hurt and I helped to look after you.'

Harris stared again.

'You want the wheel?' he said. 'The locks and chains? You want to see the needles and the pins stuck in?'

He dropped the coins into his pocket. He made a fist, and stubbed out the cigarette on the back of his hand, laughing as he screwed the cigarette into fragments, leaving the skin black with ash. He wiped it away with his sleeve.

He opened his sack, plunged his hand inside. He took out a packet of safety pins, rolled back his left sleeve, exposing tiny wounds and bruises, a tattoo of a snake wrapped round a bare tree. He began pressing the points into his flesh, pushing until the points emerged again, closing the clasps. When Tom's father recoiled, said, 'We don't want that, Harris. We don't want anything,' Harris just smiled, sighed. 'Just this one,' he said. 'And this, this...'

'Do you remember Cairo, Harris? The desert? The heat?'

'What now? The locks and chains? Or something new? Something worse, something crueller..? This maybe?' Pulling out from his sack a large fish hook attached to a piece of twine. 'Or these?' A hammer, some tweezers, a little saw.

'Nothing, Harris.'

Harris' hand reached out again.

'Time to pay again. You and the squirt there. Time to pay.'

'We don't want it, Harris.'

'Get your loot and pay.'

'You remember nothing, Harris?'

Harris stood up now and came at them.

'Think it's over but it's not. Always something else to get through. Always something else to pay for. Get your cash. You, and you and all.'

They backed off, out into the sleet again. Beneath the bridge, a small knot of spectators stood watching, sniggering. Harris laughed at them, yelled at them to pay, suddenly reached out, caught Tom's collar.

'The pretty one,' he said, and he stared out into the sleet, towards the stalls. 'Where's that one? Where's the pretty one?'

Tom recoiled, struggled to free himself.

'Not her and all?' said Harris, and his face contorted as if only now could he feel his pain.

'At home,' said Tom. 'Couldn't come.'

'At home,' said Harris and his grip relaxed, Tom pulled

away. 'Safe at home. Tucked up safe at home.'

He went back into the shelter of the bridge, began pulling the pins out from his flesh. He shuddered. 'Cold these days,' he said, glancing at Tom's father. 'So fucking cold.' He moved back towards his belongings and crouched there, began assembling his cane and money bag. 'But them days,' he said. 'Them hot days.' He stood again, turned round. 'And between them days and these days...'

Tom's father caught him by the elbow, stood close to him. 'What?' he asked.

'So hot. So fucking hot. But between them and these...'

And for a moment there was silence, Tom staring at the two men together on the quay, little Harris, ragged and confused, his father bowed over him, moving closer, the two men facing each other as if about to embrace.

'Harris,' whispered his father. 'What can I do?'

Harris pulled away, with,

'Nothing. Nothing.'

And he made his rush at the new spectators, yelling,

'You! I seen you! You been watching and you didn't pay! And you! And you and all...'

They hurried to the station through the sleet. Still early afternoon, but with the clouds so low the streets were darkening. The newspaper-seller was backed deep into a doorway. He flourished a headline at them as they passed. 'Get your shelters dug!' he yelled, furious. 'Get home and get yourselves prepared!'

'Poor Harris,' said his father in the station. 'I hardly knew him, just came across him at the end, the journey home. By that time he'd lost everything. Already too far gone.'

They leaned close together, watching.

'This one,' they said.

'The next one.'

'I'll close my eyes. I'll count to ten.'

'One and one millionth...'

'Millionths!'

His father pointed to the monument outside.

'See how the angel's getting ready to carry them up? See the dying reaching out to her? See the survivors facing outwards, guns raised, still prepared.' Tom peered, screwed up his eyes, distinguished only a heap with the angel silhouetted high above. 'Don't believe it, Tom. I saw no angels. What happened to Harris's angel? Where's the angels now, leaning down to help?'

Tom leaned closer.

'Will there be another war?'

'What's war? Maybe this is war, still going on. Maybe it's just a longer pause than usual in the fighting. Time to lick the wounds, clean the kit, count the ammo. Maybe when it all starts up again it'll be the same war, the one we thought we'd left behind, and all this time it's just been waiting, biding its time. Maybe there's only ever been one war, all the time getting bigger, nastier. There's them that want it, Tom. There's them can't wait for it.'

Their bus arrived, they climbed inside. They were silent, until after the city, out in the dark, among the fields, when Tom went on.

'You said it might just be nothing.'

'It might, Tom.'

'You said it was just a game.'

The man put his arm around the boy, drew him close.

'It is. And maybe we will survive. Maybe we will get through... It's just that between what happened then and what's happening now, between that and this, there was a time when everything seemed possible, when we seemed like children again, a time that really was a kind of heaven...'

And Tom nodded, closed his eyes, saw the calm surface of Derwent Water, the summits of Catbells and Skiddaw shimmering in the summer heat, felt her breath on his cheek, hair on his throat, was surrounded by her scent...

As they approached the village, he opened his eyes. He remained bent over, resting on the coarse damp herringbone, felt the lift of his father's chest, its sighing.

'What's wrong with her?' he said.

'Nothing's wrong.' The words came too quickly, far too quickly.

'What's wrong with her?'

Long silence, then,

'Nothing, Tom. Nothing.'

'Where've you been? Where've my two men been? Just look at you, so brave and cold!'

She fussed at them, unbuttoned their coats for them, kept exclaiming at the cold and damp they'd carried in.

'You shouldn't've gone. Soon as you went I knew you shouldn't, not the way it turned. Awful, awful.'

The house was filled with warmth – her cooking all day long, a fire blazing. She drew chairs to the fire for them. She brought them dry socks and trousers, laughed at them as they bumped into each other, changing. They ate from trays balanced on their knees, all of them gathered at the hearth. Her stew with crisp dumplings, buttery carrots, bright spinach. She kept asking about Harris, poor Harris. 'Poor soul,' said her husband. 'I think he's a long way gone.' She sighed, clicked her tongue. 'We'll have to keep on going to him. We'll give him lots of pennies. We'll try to talk to him, try to get him to see there's other ways, better ways. So sad, Tom? Still cold, I think. Tired and cold.' She brought warm cake, poured sauce on it. 'Yes?' she asked. 'Yes? You can taste the honey in it? So sweet, so warm. Catch every last drop of it, hold it on your tongue a moment more, a moment more. Feel it, Tom, driving out the cold...'

After the food, they kept the television off, the radio off. They sat there in the warmth, listening to the sleet outside and the turning of the sea, their occasional murmurings of content. Tom slept first, and he heard the spectators yelling: Get the chains on! Get the bloody skewer in!

'You're snoring,' she said. 'Just like you used to years ago.' She placed a hot water bottle in his lap, touched his tongue with her finger, a tiny drop of honey on it.

'Upstairs,' she told him. 'Upstairs, get ready.'

She guided him to the door, he heard them laughing as he went up.

The sleet had stopped. The clouds were clearing. Tom left his

David Almond

bed, watched. Moment by moment, more of the Archer was
exposed. He stood tall and unmoving over the horizon. How
long would it be until the stars dispersed, until the arrow was
released? He shuddered. Frost was beginning to form on the
window. He closed his eyes, focused deep into the darkness,
listened. The sea turned, they gasped and sighed. Was that
her cry of pain?

He stared at the stars again, their reflections on the sea.

He imagined bombers, their huge shadows moving across
the stars.

He whispered, 'When will it begin?'

As he turned to the bed again, the needle pierced his heel.
He stifled his cry, squeezed back his tears, lay on his bed and
pulled it out. Would her pain be similar to this, would she
have to calm it, moment by moment? What would happen
when she could not calm it, when there was no peace?

He took the needle, rested its point on his forearm,
waited, trembling. Would her fear be similar to this? He
pressed, harder, felt the needle breaking through his skin.

'I feel nothing,' he whispered. 'I'm fine... It's nothing,
nothing...'

LUCY BLUE

I'D NOT SEEN LUCY BLUE FOR YEARS, AND THEN THE PARCEL CAME: the key to her house, the sharpened knife, the scribbled note: Key will let you in. Knife will end it. Please come to me. Set me free.

Lucy Blue. We were children together. We were little girls with skirts tucked into our knickers splashing in the surf. She lived with her mother in a timber house way out on the headland. Beside them was the lighthouse whose light brilliantly swept the world at night. Beyond them was the cold Northumbrian sea, its chain of islands stretching to the horizon.

Her father was far away, and had been since she was born. She said he was a pirate chief swashbuckling his way across the hot seas of the south. When he sailed back he'd be laden with jewels and exotic fruits for us, he'd bring monkeys to play in the dunes and parrots to whistle in the pines. He'd take us away beyond the islands in his gorgeous sailing ship.

Sometimes as the dusk gathered and the lighthouse light began to spin, as I prepared to make my way back along the shore to my dull village, she'd grip me tight:

If you love me you'll believe me. It will be like that. You'll see.

She waited and the years passed. Her mother painted the

house as white as the lighthouse. She had cables laid from the village and switches and power points and dangling bulbs installed in every room. She laughed with Lucy:

We'll make sure he won't miss us when he comes sailing in!

And then at last he came, and we saw, and Lucy and I were children no longer. He was ragged and hunched, his face was blackened with stubble and rage. There was cider in his pockets and slurred curses on his tongue. He reeled from his wife and drooled and smacked his lips for the pretty little thing he'd spawned.

And when I felt his gaze fall upon me I scurried homeward through the dunes.

In the village, there were rumours of drug smuggling, and jail sentences in distant places. The people turned their backs to him. One day in The Angel there was a knife fight and one of the village hard boys was cut from cheek to chin. When they came to the headland at dusk to wreak revenge, the man's venom as he ran at them sent them fleeing as if from Hell.

I was forbidden to go there. At night I peered from my window. I watched the miles-long wedge of light sweeping the sea, the land, the sea again. As it passed, I squeezed my eyes against its glare. I tried to discern the glow of Lucy's house above the dunes. I prayed. I cried for her. I whispered to her, as if there were another cable linking her life to mine.

Lucy, I think of you still. Lucy, I love you still.

But more time passed, I felt myself growing away from her, my mind was drawn by other things.

And then we learned of the fate of her mother. She was lifted in a trawl net with her skull broken and with stones packed into the lining of her winter coat. Two detectives from Tyneside came to the village, went out to Lucy's place, returned without her father. They took lunch in The Angel and shrugged at all the questions. There was nothing on the man, they murmured. And they drove away.

After the funeral I went out there again. Lucy wore white like a bride and she told me that her mother had not really gone. She told me to stay until dark and see. All afternoon, I held her hand at the table.

Lucy, I whispered. Come back with me!

From deeper in the house came the muttering and cursing of her father, his snores, his whimperings, his calling from the depths of awful dreams. He lurched into the doorway at dusk, grunting some praise of the pretty little girls of Bangkok and Ceylon.

Lucy, I whispered. Come back with me!

He staggered closer. I saw the knife shoved down inside his belt. I smelt his livid breath. His eyes reeled and his tongue rolled on his lips as he reached for me.

I ran home weeping through the swinging floods of light.

When I next went back I found her sitting on the shore. All around her were scattered switches and power points and bulbs. Electric cables and wire were tangled in the heaped-up weed. She laughed and told me it was better this way. He'd ripped out everything. He'd said he couldn't bear to have light getting everywhere, exposing everything. She giggled

57

and held me, and drew me to the house. He was wrong, she said. It's the light that blocks out everything. If I came inside and waited until dark, I'd truly see.

Inside were the scents of candles and burned paraffin. Again his whisperings and cries from further in. I held my friend, I gazed into her eyes.

Lucy, I whispered. Come back with me.

She smiled. We waited. I wept for the life that was being drained from her and she stroked my hand in order to comfort me.

Soon the lighthouse light began its pulse: long periods of dark and sudden bursts of light. I must just relax, she said. I must gaze about me in the room. I must allow myself to see. Outside, the darkness deepened. I imagined the long stretch of shore between me and my home. I trembled and she soothed me: it was all right, everything was all right. Wait until the light had passed and focus on the dark. The dark, each time a little darker. Soon I'd see.

There! she gasped. There!

She gripped me, nails biting my flesh.

There! You have to see her! There!

I stared across the table. The white flare of Lucy's face and dress plunged in and out of dark. Her eyes swivelled, she glared through me and past me and at me.

Oh, see! she begged me. Please see!

I heard him coming through the house.

Lucy! Please come back with me!

The door swung open and I ran.

And didn't stop running until I'd made a future for myself

that was nothing to do with this place, and nothing to do with Lucy Blue. And then, as if they had pursued me ever since that night: the key, the knife, the note: Key will let you in. Knife will end it. Please...

It was a day-long journey. I drove to the village, the dull place. I parked outside The Angel. I trudged through the dunes to the shore. The falling sun lit up the house and lighthouse way out on the headland. All along the beach were stinking heaps of weed and stranded jellyfish, the endless line of waste thrown up by the sea. The sea itself was hardly moving, it was oily and flat, lazily slopping against itself where it met the shore. Not a soul to be seen. Closer to, I saw how Lucy's mother's paint had begun to peel away, how the timbers had distorted and cracked. Doors and windows were tight shut. I thought of calling but the words just gurgled in my throat. There were footprints in the sand, but leading everywhere, no way of learning anything from them.

I reached for the door and my heart began to thunder and the world grew dark. Locked. I whimpered, taking the key, inserting it, turning it. Shuddering as I did, I nicked my skin, caused drops of blood on the key, the door, the handle.

Oh, Lucy! I prayed. Just come outside. Come back with me.

I turned the handle and went inside. The table as always. The candle and paraffin scents. The scent of the man: alcohol, bitterness and sweat. I stood in a corner of the room beside the door. The name I would cry still gurgled uselessly in my throat. From outside came the final screaming of the gulls as the light began to turn.

Lucy! I whispered. Where are you, Lucy?

But nothing, just time plunging onwards, intensifying the darkness, intensifying the light. I felt my tears running, heard the draughts in the timbers, the turning sea, something shuffling somewhere on the sand. I steeled myself, I gripped the handle of the knife, I stared into the dark, each time a little darker.

Lucy! Where are you, Lucy? I've come to see you, Lucy...

And then there she was, so sudden and so clear, in the opposite dark corner – the white bloom of her bridal dress, her smiling eyes in the white bloom of her face.

Oh, Lucy! I gasped, and I reached towards her. Come back with me, Lucy!

She disappeared in the pulse of light, reappeared in the stretch of dark.

Her lips opened and closed as if to welcome me but no sound came.

What is it, Lucy?

She drew back the collar of her dress, showed me the bruises and the lacerations, and then she smiled again, so joyous, and I began to see beside her the other woman, more obscure in her dark winter coat, and my heart leapt, and I said.

Oh, Lucy! I see! I truly see!

I moved towards them, but as I moved the light turned once more and showed me the man approaching on the beach.

I stepped back into the dark behind the door. I smiled

across at my friend. I raised the sharpened knife. I waited for
him to enter, this false pirate chief, this father, this fiend...

FIRES

THE HOT YEAR, LATE MAY, AND ALREADY THE MOORS ABOVE THE TOWN are bleached and baked. Already there've been fires there. Already we're commanded to be frugal, to bathe less often, neglect our gardens. The river in town is dark and sluggish between crazed banks. Scent of drains pervades the streets. Out here everything is stunted. Flies swarm in the archway of hedge above the gate. The leaves of father's dahlias wither as they open.

'We've buggered it,' he tells me. I'm in the deck chair, Holy Sonnets in my lap, crib notes scattered on the earth around me. 'What did they expect? The world'd keep on taking it and taking it? Man so proud, war upon war, poison belching everywhere. It's getting its own back now. Turning us to desert. It's cursing us.'

I laugh at that. 'It's only summer, father.' Look at how brown I am, feel the freedom of nothing but flimsy frocks and sandals. 'We should be glad of it. This is what summer's like in places where they have a summer.'

He crouches at a border filled with marigolds – all bright flower burning, no foliage – and sifts the parched dirt between his fingers. The uneven set of his shoulders, the crackle of his breath. The thought that comes unbidden more and more as I grow older: I should have known you earlier, before you aged, years before I came.

'That's where you'll be going?' he says. 'When you've left us? Places where there's summer.'

Hang my head. No answer. Already spent so many tears in answering him. Hear his breath spat out, and soon he passes me – the dragging of his legs, black trousers, black boots strapped tight – heading to the back of the house, the shade. From there his call, more of sadness than of anger.

'And put some bloody clothes on, will you? There's too much of that Lisa in you now...'

Lisa. She comes in through the arched hedge minutes later. Hair shimmers as she clears the flies, sun high above the moors bathes her in light. The books she carries are cumbersome things, they thump onto the lawn...

'Damned weather,' she laughs. 'Why's it always summer? Why can't the bastards test us in the winter, in the cold and dark?'

'To keep us tame. Stop us stripping off and dancing across the moors.'

'Which we'd do.'

'Which we'd do.'

Kneels before me, face fills with despair.

'God, Jenny,' she whispers. 'What'll I do?'

Close my books, spread my fingers through her hair, begin to stroke and soothe her. Wait for her to start, for the familiar words to start...

'Can't. Just can't, Jenny. Can't even start to know what it's supposed to mean. So difficult, so...'

Touch the tears on her cheek. Always the same, ever since

our first day at school, when she clung to me, and wept and begged all day for me to take her home.

She grabs my hands, holds them at her skull.

'Empty,' she says. 'Head full of nothing. Head full of air.'

'You'll pass. You passed before.'

'Cause you trained me, got me chanting every word I'd need to know. All those evenings...'

Those evenings, till my father came in yelling. Nothing the dolt could learn for herself? Needed stuffing, force-feeding, cramming? Needed to suck my brains, lap up my words? He gripped the back of my chair, hauled me from her. Stop feeding her. Starve her. Empty little thing. She'll come to nothing. She's nothing to you. Bugger all...

Turn her, hold her lovely face in my hands. Begin to speak but she spreads her hand across my mouth.

'No, Jenny. No comfort. It's coming to an end. I'll fail, I'll stay, and you'll be leaving. And when you come back you'll have changed, you'll have grown beyond all this. Won't know how to speak to me, till you'll see at last how I am, and always was, and how stupid it is to keep trying, till you just stop coming back at all.'

'No, Lisa,'

'That's how it'll be.'

Look down, seek comfort.

'John's staying.'

'Yes, Jenny.' Stare at each other. John. Round-faced, black-haired, scrupulous and serious John. 'And who's to know what that might bring.'

My father, his feet on the narrow path at the house's

side. She releases herself, shuffles away, sits with book on her closed knees, is studious and intent. He stands there watching from the shade. Detest him for this – that my beautiful friend should be forced to bow her head politely to the words that trip her up: Despaire behind... death before... Such terrour, and my feeble flesh doth waste... There are blackbirds in the hedges, singing, singing. Use their noise to cover me, whisper, 'So beautiful. Most lovely friend. Best I shall ever know. Best I ever want to know...'

Soon, we leave the garden and the books. Head for the open country at the street's end, where the roadway fades to a narrow cindered track and the gardens are fenced from gorse and turf and heather. The larks lift before us, climb and hang high over us, fill the air with their cries. We follow narrow rabbit-forged runs among the heather. The sun blazes, the parched peat trembles beneath our feet. Miles of moor fill the foreground, mount to the sky.

'Could never abandon this.' I say. 'Imagine never seeing this again, never doing this again.'

Higher up, we rest on turf. Heather filled with bees. The scent of blossom, scorched scent of recent fires. She lies upon me, I cradle her head to my breast. Below us the dense town, its pall of smoke filling the valley. From somewhere nearby the noise of children, then silence. Fondle her hair, feel her hand upon my calf. Close my eyes, recall our children's games by the remote pool, when we sat in close, triangular, looked at each other, inspected each other. Saw right from the start how Lisa drew John's eyes, how he looked at me with curiosity, but when he turned to Lisa, something further enticed him, something further burned in his eyes. That warm summer we spent whole afternoons naked on the turf and in the stream, sheltered stock-still amongst the gorse whenever hikers or other children passed our way, until in each of us suddenly the changes started – tiny hairs, bulbs of breasts, shyness and covertness – and we moved to other ways of being together and free above the town: long hikes across the tops; picnics; intense discussions of the failings of those we had left below. Not till years later did Lisa tell me that the game continued without me into the autumn, that on a cold bright afternoon in September he rested his still-tiny penis in her palm and told her, 'It's for when we're married, Lisa. I'll put it inside you and hold you tight and we'll never part. Never.'

'Lisa,' I whisper. 'Even if you don't pass ...'

'When I don't pass...'

'You could leave anyway. You could come with me.'

'That old tale.'

'Yes, that old tale. Going together, making it together...'

'World beneath our feet, footloose and free.'

'Yes, Lisa. Yes.'

'And where's me in this? Some grubby office job while you swan round all arty and studenty. Oh yes, my pal from the sticks – childhood promise, you know. Looks nice but not much there, no, not much there...'

'You'd make it.'

'Ha!'

'With your looks...'

'My looks, my body, all I've ever known. Brains is fair

enough, sweetheart, as my mum says, but beauty's what they're looking for. Some comfort, eh?'

'It's true, though. In a way.'

'In a way. In the way they strip you with their eyes and the way they dream you laid out helpless, ready and waiting. Not counting the ones, like your dad, that see something to be hated, something to drive them wild...'

'Not hate, Lisa,'

'No? What about the tales that's told, the whispers. That's the one, that swanky one. Tits at ten and hips like a whore at twelve. Look at the face think butter wouldn't melt, but see that body, see the way it moves...'

Hold her close. She goes on.

'Love to get it. Love to shag it. Love, love, lovely. Hate's what they mean.'

Hold her tight, so tight. Cling to her. Imagine entering her, breaking through her skin, becoming one body with her, pain and pain cancelling each other out, joy and joy redoubling.

'Thought we'd go on for ever,' she says. 'Thought we'd never change. Stupid, you see. Stupid empty little thing.'

'Beautiful,' I whisper. 'Lovely thing. If I were you. If only I were you...'

*

'Like gold to ayery thinnesse beat?' she says. 'Ayery thinnesse? The things they make you read.'

I am with my mother, I test my quotes on her.

'A very thinnesse,' I say. 'Thin as air. To turn a metal, gold, by beating it, to something insubstantial as air. Gold as a symbol of the spirit, the shining lightness inside us all. The theory that one piece of metal could be beaten and expanded infinitely, one piece of gold turned to leaf that could cover the whole world. Imagine it. A gilded world, everything squalid obscured by the shining skin. A world in which souls might meet and mingle. Our two soules therefore which are one, though I must goe, endure not yet a breach...'

She raises her hands in submission.

'Listen to you,' she says. 'Where you get it from I'll never know.'

'From thin air. But I'll save all that. Unnecessary speculation, they'll call it. I'll write my quotes, my neat essays, and I'll pass. And you'll be proud of me. Even if he isn't. Even if he hates me for it.'

'It's love, my love. Love too fierce if the truth be told. But yes, I'll be proud of you. Never been anything but proud.'

It's late evening. The house dead still, the windows open. A blackbird sings, heads for the last time to its nest. Hear him outside, now the sun is gone, pouring the liquids we've collected all day long – water from washbasin and sink, unused tea – into his borders. See him stooping, dipping cup into pail, trickling the dark mixture onto the roots of his dahlias.

'Fanatical,' she whispers. 'Better concreted over in this weather.'

'Be lost without it.'

'Specially once you've gone on your way.'

I touch my quotes. 'Another?'

'Another.'

'Prompt me, then.'

'The world's...'

'...whole sap is sunke: The generall balme th'hydroptique earth... John!'

She raises her eyes.

'There,' I say. 'Out there, look.'

He's entered the garden, squats by my father. Their low voices, the way they gently touch the leaves together.

She smiles, 'If we'd've had a son, he used to say. You've come to the right place for testing!' she calls. 'Goe! Goe, and catche! What's next?'

He comes grinning.

'Well?' she says. 'Our Jenny knows them all!'

'A falling starre.' He leans on the sill. 'Goe and catche a falling starre, Get with child a mandrake roote, Tell me where all past yeares are, Or who cleft the Divel's foot; Teach me to...'

'Pass. Ten out of ten. Get that lad to university.'

'Always was a swot,' I say.

'I'm walking,' he says.

See the yearning in his eyes.

'Yes.' I say. 'I've done enough.'

Out into the dusk. The town fills the valley and the northern sky with its light. The moors are black. Above them a handful of the strongest stars. We sit at the street's end, on a steel bench next to the cindered track.

'I love this place,' I say. 'Moving so quickly from town to

wilderness. Silence that's never true silence but always has
the noise of engines in it. Darkness and the light. You know?'

'I know.'

'Like the body and the soul, the meeting point between
the body and the soul.'

'Too much Donne, Jenny. Too much swotting.'

'Hold my hand, John, Hold me down. That's better.'

We lean together. Imagine leaving, turning to wave,
suddenly adult. Feel the steady rise and fall of John's chest,
stare into the gathering dark. What would there be to replace
all this?

'Went to see Lisa earlier,' he says. 'Her mother wouldn't
let me in. Said she was with you. I knew she wasn't.'

'No'

'Walked up the hill towards you. Kept seeing how things
will be. You gone. Lisa and me still here. Me more bitter by
the week. Lisa more aloof. How we'll despise each other,
damage each other. After all we've been through, all we've
shared.'

'Change your mind, John. Go somewhere else. You could
go anywhere.'

'Freedom, eh?'

'Freedom. It's not an empty word.'

'No such thing. Not now, not yet, not till what will
happen has happened and we're properly thrown together or
properly thrown apart. Her avoiding me's no good. Just puts
off everything.'

'She avoids you because she loves you, John. Childhood
love. Friendship love. Like you and me love.'

'Isn't like that, not with Lisa. It's something else – dreaming her, hunting her, wanting her to the exclusion of all others.'

'She didn't want that, John.'

'Wanting's nothing. Whatever she wants I've got this thing that keeps on burning, and till she comes to me it's like being in hell all alone, being roasted all alone.'

'Now who has too much Donne?'

'You don't understand. Love isn't just a gentle little thing or an aching yearning thing. Sometimes it's fierce and full of hate.'

Tremble, hearing again the opposites so close.

'Hate?'

'For the thing I used to love. Her beauty made me love her first, but now I do love her it's her beauty keeps us apart. Her beauty isn't her. Her beauty keeps her from me. It's her beauty that I hate.'

'John. Oh, John.'

'Don't you see? If she was ordinary, plain. If she was any ordinary-looking girl. Then she'd be glad of me. But no, she can have any man, any time, any of the men that watch her, want to touch her, want her for themselves. No need of me. Sometimes when I'm watching her or dreaming her, I see her with the beauty ruined, gone, and with her plain and ordinary and wanted just by me.'

Leave the bench, walk by the garden hedges. Keep his hand in mine, feel him burning. Keep stopping him, hugging him, trying to soothe him.

'You can never say how things might have been,' I say.

'There's only how they are. She won't come to you, not the way you want her to.'

'She'll see it's right. She'll see it's how things must be. Or what's it been for? All these years...'

Give up on him.

'I'm going in. I need to sleep.'

We stand at the gate, the arched hedge.

'In the dark it's worse,' I say. 'In the morning you'll be better.'

He pulls me to him, I catch my breath, feel his arms around me.

'Jenny,' he says. 'There must be others. Tell me.'

'John.'

He won't let me go.

'Must be others. Looks like that, body like that.'

'Let go, John.'

'She went wrong, Jenny. Went astray. Like your dad says...'

'My dad!'

'Yes like he's always said...'

Grab at him, but he's gone, running into the congested valley. Enter the garden. The windows are blazing with light.

2

Gentle morning, 7.30, street dead still, blackbirds singing in the hedges. A night of torment: numberless souls streaming from the horizon, scattered bodies rising from the turf, blast of trumpets filling the air. In my night gown I stare out:

garden then street then moors then sky then sun. A plain world, an ordinary world, but the torments continue, just words now. Shudder, seeing my nakedness obscured as I pull the elements of the dark uniform over me. Inside me, stanza after stanza taking its shape, running its course. I am well prepared, yet I tremble. Downstairs at the table a knife slips, cuts my finger, spills blood on my plate. Gather my things, leave the red droplet on the white porcelain, hear my parents wishing me well.

Down into the valley, through long steepening streets, the waking town, towards the slow river. Hesitate on the bridge, lean on the parapet, watch the dark water, thin slick between dark banks. Far to the east the high arch of the city's bridge shines dully in the early light. On through the shopping streets, small centre of this place, tawdry shop fronts hoisted over ancient brick and stone. Smell bread baking, bacon frying. A train squeals in our small station. Through a park where the annuals flop among flourishing weeds. Noise of motors and engines, somewhere a boy hawking newspapers, somewhere a dog in frenzy.

Hurry on, knowing I'll be leaving this, I'll move beyond all this.

School gleams from beyond the park, all around it acres of beaten bleached grass. Follow the chain link fence, seek the entrance, find it where posts are uprooted and ripped free, where the fence is a knee-high squash of grey metal. Step through, approach the building, stare up in surprise at the singing of a lark, so rare down here away from the safer nesting-places of the moors, see it hang a hundred feet above, trembling dark point against the blue, and feel it hangs there just for me, sings just for me, is familiar just to me. Wave my arm, acknowledge its presence, whisper,

'Lark. Joy. My singing soul.'

After the weeks of preparation at home, released from this place to wear thin frocks, to go barelegged, I move stiffly, awkwardly. Moving closer, through the children already gathered, I tense my spine, hold my head erect as voices call me. Privileged ones, treated to kindly gestures from the staff, we to be tested are let inside and we stand there nervous, pale-faced, giggling. The gymnasium's laid out for us with long neat rows of desks. Keep turning to the mocking throng outside, watch for John or Lisa coming through, but we're taken in, guided to our places, are already being hushed, told to sit, compose ourselves before John is at my shoulder staring at me, speechless, some ecstasy burning from him. Reach out to him but he is ordered to his own place yards in front of me. As the papers are distributed, keep turning, turning, but she's nowhere to be seen, and John is dead still, leaning at his desk, all prepared.

Sit for minutes in the silence, unable to begin, until at last the stanzas come and as the sun beats through the wide windows down at me, dazing me with heat and light, I write of the poet's loves for God and women, how they are the same love, that strips the world of its vestments, reaches through naked words towards the soul.

And lift my head, watch for her again. Hasn't come. Grab a teacher's arm as he walks past.

'Where is she? What's happened to my friend?'

An ironic smile, a careless shrug: Surprised? Really surprised?

'Look after yourself now, Jennifer.' Eyes that suggest the whispered words are filled with wisdom. 'Only yourself...'

Out in the dark corridor again, John controls me. Others are calling me, wanting me.

'Where's Lisa?' I'm asked. 'What's happened to her?'

But John takes me, leads me to the fence, turns me to the town. Abandon myself to him, let myself be led by him. Only at the bridge where we hesitate, gasp,

'Where is she, John? What's happened to her?'

'Backed off. Didn't have the heart for it.' Holds me so tight. 'You, Jenny. You'll get her for me.'

Move again, this time into Lisa's estate. Now he doesn't hold my hand. Follow, dog, pursue him. On either side, low garden walls, gardens, pebbledashed facades. Children in a garden, wild in a paddling pool, pack of dogs with tongues hanging low eyeing them. Car without wheels, resting on bricks, oil stains soaked deep into the pale road. Music blaring from open windows, wide-open doors. On a low wall, men stripped to the waist, gesticulating at each other. The heat fierce, light glaring on the pale facades. We approach her house, he hesitates again. See the tears in his eyes.

'She said it was always wrong. I was always in the way. It isn't true.'

Stares into my eyes.

'It isn't true!'

'It isn't true.' I answer.

Draw him forward, hand in hand.

'We'll talk with her,' I say. 'We'll sort it out.'

Mock leaded panes, plastic curtain hanging before the opened front door. Little dried-out fish pond in the front garden, garish blue plastic in the dust. Inside the front window the bird cage, the canary, its brilliant singing as we approach. His hand tightens. Tap the door frame with clenched fist, shudder. How did we get to this?

'Lisa,' I call, 'Lisa.'

No answer.

'She's in there.'

'Lisa?' I call.

He shoves through the curtain.

The place as it has always been. On shelves and sills and tables little glass ornaments, sea creatures, bright animals on frail legs. Fringed rugs, fringes hanging from the edges of upholstery. Mirrors, frames gilded in imitation of foliage.

Everything open: all windows, all doors. Air moving gently through the house, carrying perfume, disinfectant, scent of freshly cut oranges. The canary singing, singing from its cage.

'There,' says John, 'There. Look.'

Through the back window see sun loungers beneath high hedges. A low table bearing oranges, a bottle of wine. Magazines strewn across the ground. An arm stretched out, a knee raised. Hear the low rattle in John's throat.

Step quietly on the grass. Straightaway know we were wrong, it isn't Lisa, she isn't there. It is her mother who sits up and turns to us, gives her familiar indulgent smile, sits there with arm lifted to cover her bare breasts.

'Well?' she says, and beams. 'Well? And how was it, my loves?'

John's face is burning. Words tangled in his throat. Lisa's mother draws a towel across herself.

'Jenny?'

'It's you,' says John. 'You. Has been all along. Twisting her from the start. Just got to look at her, look at you. Little doll, little whore. You, you, legs spread, tits out. You're the one. It's fucking you...'

Hold him tight, grip him.

'John. Oh, John.'

'It's true. Mother whore and daughter whore.'

'She didn't come.' I say. 'Just didn't come.'

Realise I am crying, an infant again. See John running to the house, quitting this place. She stands and takes me in her arms.

'The silly girl,' she says. 'She said she couldn't go. I said she must. But who am I to listen to? Don't, Jenny. Don't, my love. She always said she wouldn't pass.'

A door slams, feet drum on the pavement. See John in the gap between the houses, running from the estate.

'Forgive him,' I say. 'He's wild for her. He'd die for her.'

'I know that. Saw it ages back. He's been coming here at night. She doesn't want him in. Won't go away. Stays there prowling, waiting for her. Then again this morning, till the last minute, till he had to go. Poor boy. Too intense. Nothing's worth all this. Poor all of you.'

Say I'll have to follow him. She holds me closer.

'Just let them go.'

'Can't let them do this to each other.'

She laughs, so tender, lays her hand so gently on my cheek.

'Do what? It's only love and all the rotten things that go with love. They're learning early, that's all. If I were you, I'd get those awful things off, stretch out in the sun, let them get on with it.'

But can't do that. Pull free of her. From the gate, look back. She stands there with her arm still raised across her breasts, hair fallen free of its clips, smile of gentle irony on her face. Slender, at ease with her body, bathed in sun. If I were you. If I were you...

I turn into the glare again.

Halfway there, find father coming down. Shelter in an alley, deep into overhanging honeysuckle. Through the foliage watch him pass. The dark suit, the heavy, stiff-legged walk. The neck taut, the head held forward, even from this distance the relentless forward-looking eyes. Once as a child, touching through his clothes the leather corset at his waist, the steel plate on his thigh, asked him, What happened, daddy? What did this to you? Angrily he threw me off, I sprawled across the floor. He lifted me tenderly. Through tears he whispered, Nothing did it, my little love. And later, more reflective, as I lay in silence on his lap, falling to sleep: Don't look back, my love. Never look back. Then years later found out of course it was war, years before I was born.

Run uphill. John nowhere in sight. Lunchtime. Imperceptibly moving air. The pavement giving back heat. The smells of food frying, bubbling fat. The moors shimmering. In our street breathe heavily. Tug at my collar, the waist of my heavy skirt. Try to recall the morning, try to recall one sentence I've written, but all's gone, evaporated by the heat, and I feel despair. Have I wasted myself in thoughts of my friends? Have I let them hold me back? Yearn to leap forward, be carried from this place into my new and independent world, to be free of this torment. I will stay in the garden, continue to prepare myself. A month of examinations, of biding time, then breaking loose.

Mother sighs, seeing my exhaustion.

'Poor angel. You'll have sailed it. Just you wait and see.'

She has given me food, small bowl of salad and bread, allowed me to eat, before, with bitterness in her voice, 'Your chum's upstairs.'

She nods.

'Stupid child. The stupid, stupid child.'

She is on the bed, a magazine in her lap. She's been sleeping, is just waking.

'Dreamed you'd gone,' she says. 'There'd been fighting, a war somewhere. Everything ruined. How you must hate me.'

Don't answer. Stand at the window, try to imagine how I might feel.

'Jenny. Send me away, Once and for all, get rid of me.'

See John, high up, coming down through blackened heather.

'I love you,' I whisper. 'I'm part of you. You know that.'

Begin undressing, let the uniform thump to the floor, sigh,

'God. When it's all over, when it's all done.'

Pull on the frock, the sandals. Stare into a mirror, see how my hair has grown this year, how it hangs heavy on my shoulders. Search my face, seek new beauty caused by weeks of sun, something adult in the shape or the expression.

'How was it?' she asks.

Shake my head.

'Like a dream. Can't tell. Can hardly remember.' See her, stretched out on the bed, so graceful. 'Kept watching for you. Right to the last minute, I thought you'd come.'

'I was coming. Honest I was. Then I saw him waiting. The look in his eyes. The way he just stood there. It wasn't him. I should have ignored him, run past him. But I couldn't. Was scared anyway. What would I have written? Come on, then, he was saying. Come on, then, bitch. A challenge. Nothing like him, not him. Turned away, started running, heard him laughing... Feel ashamed, Jenny. Should I be?'

Shrug. All these years. Maybe all I've wanted is to make her some more desirable version of myself.

'Doesn't matter. It was never you.'

Press my finger to my lips, go downstairs. Tell my mother that John will come. She must tell him Lisa isn't here. I'll deal with him.

'She must be gone before your father comes.'

'She will be.'

Upstairs again, take her hand.

'John's wild. He's looking for you. He'll come here.'

'I couldn't face him.'

'He won't know.'

Lean down, kiss her.

'Do you remember,' I say. 'A hundred years ago when we pricked our fingers with needles and pressed the wounds together?'

She laughs.

'Blood sisters. How we giggled and licked each other's blood away?'

'And then how solemn we were so suddenly.'

'I remember.'

'It hasn't changed. There's still you in me and me in you. I'd still protect you to the death.'

Lean down and hold her, hear him in the garden, at the door, hear him repeating her name, demanding her.

'Stay till we're away,' I tell her. 'Then go home. I'll try to calm him.'

He's at the kitchen door, is flushed, bloodshot eyes.

'She isn't here,' I say.

'I've told him,' she says.

He glares at me. See how close he is to tears.

'It's true, John. She isn't here.'

He's filthy. Shoes and trousers coated with ash from the moors. Hands blackened; he must have been on all fours. Reach past her towards him, rest my hand on his shoulder.

'Idiot,' I say.

Fill a basin of water, wash his hands for him. Wipe his face with tissues, comb his hair for him. For the moment he's given himself up to me, is blank-faced, impassive.

'Hey,' I say. 'Hey.' But can draw no smiling from him.

Soon I take him out. Feel in his hand how he's drawing

strength, calmness from me. Don't speak, just watch the larks lifting as we leave the street behind. The cinder track gives way to turf, gentle gradient with forked paths heading up towards the higher places. Walk by a stream, thin slow trickle in a deep ditch. Down there: brilliant mosses and weed, star-shaped blooms.

Dried-out earth shudders, feels hollowed-out. A dead frog in our path, skin shrunken and leathery. Lift it, and it's stiff, lightweight, primitive, something to be mummified a time before turning to earth again.

'My dad says this place'll turn to desert,' I say.

'Yes.'

'Water's the binding and the blood. Without it when the cold winds come the top will simply blow away. We'll be left with bare rocks, dust blowing from crevice to crevice. The bones of a place... Dead.'

He shrugs, continues walking.

'Doom and gloom,' I say. 'His doom and gloom.'

From miles away, the booming of artillery: the danger area, miles of moor cordoned-off for war games.

'Bastards,' says John.

'Yes. But listen to the larks.'

Soon there are no defined paths. Feel his agitation returning.

'Shouldn't go on,' he says. 'Should go back and find her.'

Put my arm across him, a comfort and a barrier.

'Let her be, John. Just let her be.'

Come to a hollow between two hills, a place of gorse and rabbits. Further on, a small flock of sheep. They twist their

heads towards us, stare, stupid. Another stream breaks from
a tiny crag here, trickles down into a round pool, seeps into
the earth again, evaporates.

'She doesn't care,' he says. 'It's all because she doesn't
care.'

Lead him to a pillow of turf beside a familiar pool.

'Sit for a while,' I say.

See that he is lost here. Feel how he trembles.

'John.'

Shuffle closer, take his hand, know how stupid he is made
by love. His eyes bulge, he is caught between fury and fright.
Recall Lisa's touch, the beauty of her eyes, know how her soul
is suffocated by this boy. Move closer, take his hand, lay it on
my breast. He recoils, confused.

'It's all right,' I tell him. 'It's okay.'

Draw him back to me, feel the excitement in him growing.

'Remember?' I whisper. 'All those years back. Days like
this out here before we'd grown. Yes, John? Remember,
John?'

Unbutton my frock, begin pulling it over my hips, my
waist.

'The three of us. Freed from everything down there.'

'Yes.'

He helps me lift the dress over my head. His eyes are half-
closed, his face is filled with sadness.

'I know,' I whisper. 'I know, my love.'

Lay his hand on me again. Unbutton his shirt, smile at
the little clump of hairs at the centre of his chest.

'Touch me,' I say. 'Be free with me.'

He's clumsy, confused.

'Be free,' I tell him. 'Do what you want to.'

Whisper to him.

'John. It's all right. Imagine I'm her.'

'Jenny,' he whispers.

'Lisa,' I say. 'Take off everything. Do anything you want to.'

Lie there waiting. The heat rising from beneath me, the droning of insects in the gorse and grass, the droning of distant engines. Anticipate pain and blood, some pleasure. Imagine there will be some moment of transformation, that in this place I will be lifted through an act of love from childhood confinements to adult liberties. But it is not to be. Open my eyes. He kneels over me, his body poised and beautiful, but his face tight shut, fierce, turned in on itself. Behind closed eyes, he sees Lisa, she who is not me. And groans, pulls his clothes back on, gives me a glance of despair, and leaves me there.

'Oh, John,' I whisper. 'Oh, poor John.'

And lie an age like that, naked in the heat, gaze through the astounding yellow of the gorse into the blue, surrounded by the sound of water, the insects, wild singing of the larks.

Children's laughter brings me out of it. They are on a higher slope, faces peeking over the tips of the gorse.

Laugh. Go down to the pool and sip water from cupped hands. As I dress, stand on tiptoe to wave at them. Only one of them remains, little girl, waving shyly back.

'Good morrow, wild one,' I whisper. 'Good morrow, little wild friend.'

3

Again at peace, late evening. Tenderly, from shoe boxes beneath my bed, I lift these things out. Old diaries, painstaking script of infancy giving way to teenage dash. Envelopes of pressed flowers, feathers, butterflies' wings. Eyelashes, the first false pair, that had made my father roar with rage. Milk tooth. Pink plastic ring with silver skin flaking from it. Strings and strings of buttons and beads. Matchboxes padded with cotton wool, the blown eggs of skylark, curlew, snipe. Little stones that sparkle when licked. Pebbles rounded and smoothed by running streams. Necklace of melon seeds. False fingernails. Shed skin of an adder. Tiny antler branch. In a phial, the mingled strands of hair, my brown, John's black, Lisa's blonde. There are photographs: baby me in my father's lap, spreadeagled in the garden, naked in the bath. Lisa caught in mid-dance, released from earth, hair streaming high, John eyeing her suspiciously from the archway. The three of us arranged on the lawn, all neat, hems tucked round knees, tablecloth of sandwiches and lemonade before us. Cuttings from the local paper: bonny baby Lisa in her mother's arms; Harvest Princess at the church gate, berries and golden leaves woven in her hair; Carnival Queen in her swimsuit, waving from her throne; then me all studious in my uniform, praised for my results. Sit on the floor, lean on the bed, arrange these things around me. My little shrine. Touch with fingertips, lift these things to eye and tongue to peer, squint, lick, taste and remember. Ache for these things to open in my presence, to release the true sensations of childhood. But they are icons now, little ornate windows letting through light from the past, but no means of return. Carefully replace them. Try to recall what is next. What must I turn my head to learning? From the night outside, the distant thundering of guns. A siren wailing in the valley. Think of John that afternoon, my almost-transformation. Another such moment will come soon, I'll move beyond all this. Mother calls up the stairs. Jennifer! Jennifer! Pause in mid-thought, catch my breath, and the world begins to roar, lifting me, hurling me forward.

Lisa's mother is at the table. She trembles, weeps, jerks her head at me.

'You told me it was wild,' she says. 'I said it was a little thing. You said you couldn't let them. I said just let them go.'

Father watches from the doorway.

'Tell me,' I say. 'Tell me.'

He shrugs, looks down.

'Gone too far,' he says. 'Gone stupid.'

Stammer, can't speak, can't ask, then my mother's whispering.

'Lisa's fine, my love. Everything will be fine.'

'No. No. Never never never again...'

But she is fine. Clumsy, he fumbled his assault, didn't hold her still. She held her hands before her face. The backs of her hands and her hair were splashed. Thin splashes in the gap between her hands and hairline. They've cut the burned hair away. A scorched ring frames her face. But it was a weak solution. The marks are delicate, will soon fade. Her shock will relent. She'll be fine. Sit by her bed in the hospital.

They've said she isn't ready but she demands to leave. The curtains are drawn around us. Her hands are bound with bandages. Gently, I help her with her clothes.

'Said I didn't know him,' she whispers. 'Invented someone awful, someone terrible. Middle-aged. Foul breath. Callouses on his fingers. Scars. Brutish. Beast from across the moors. Didn't believe me. They know about John's prowling. It wasn't him, I just kept saying. No. It wasn't him.'

Keep running my hands across her arms, her hips, her waist.

'How could he...?' I start, but our eyes meet. I'm silent.

'They went to find him,' she says. 'But all night he's not been home. They came back and just looked at me: and still you say it wasn't him?' Stand with her, brush her hair. Kiss her on the lips, hold her tight, feel the sobbing in her chest, taste the salt on her cheeks.

'Wasn't him,' she whispers. 'When he grabbed me and dragged me from the street he was grunting about love. He got my face between his hands and he really was the beast. It's this I hate, he said. This I fucking hate. Then he's fumbling in his pockets and getting the stuff out and jerking and whimpering. John, I say. John. But it isn't him. And I back off and hold my hands up and let him get on with it and feel the burning and hear him running, running. The fool. Silly fool...'

We wait, holding each other for so long, then part the curtains, leave the ward.

'You should be reading,' she tells me as we leave the centre, begin to climb.

'Time for that. Years of time, once I've left all this.'

A police car. It slows, the officers study us.

'They want everything,' she says. 'What he did, what he didn't do. They won't have nothing...'

'It's all we'll give them. He was with me, I'll say. Sex in the hot night. Passion all night long...'

She laughs, squeezes my hand.

'Maybe I will leave, too,' she says. 'But alone, strong as you.'

'Strong!'

The sun glares, a pall of smoke rises above the moors.

'Look, the lark,' she says, and I peer upward, letting her direct me. The bird is high above us, perched on air, piping the wild song.

Hurry on. Pass the entrance to her estate, take the alleyways that will avoid my home. Above us the sky is darkening, the scent of smoke fills the air. We break from the houses onto heather and turf. High up, the heather is burning.

She takes my hand. I feel her trembling.

'Oh, Jenny. I'm so scared.'

'Hush. These are the best days. Quaking with fear. Filled with delight.'

Move higher, towards the flames. There are sirens in the valley, moving closer. See John amongst the flames. He is crouched low, running uphill, burning torch in his hand. At intervals he hesitates, sets another tussock burning, runs uphill again. As he moves, he is obscured by the smoke, visible, obscured again. He is naked. His body is blackened by smoke and ash. Yell at him, but our voices are drowned by the crackling of fire around him. Stand stunned, marvelling. Rabbits burst from cover. A hare bounds free, swerves within feet of us. The sky is mad with larks. Behind us a small crowd has gathered at the street's end. See my father, black-suited among them, unmoving at the boundary of town and moor. A fire engine comes into sight. Two policemen on the cindered track. There is a path through the flames, a track so beaten there is nothing to burn on it. Lisa leads. We move uphill. In among the flames the air crackles and spits. Already on the lower slopes the heather has been turned to ash, the flames are diminishing. Run to the newer flames, shoulder-high in places, with John among them. 'John!' we scream. 'Oh, John!' Sparks are flying from beneath Lisa's feet. John sees us now, stares down at us from a rocky summit. Perhaps we should slow, take our time in reaching him, but the track has narrowed, the flames are close, sparks keep catching in our clothes, singeing, smouldering. We come through to the rocks, haul ourselves onto them. Cling together an instant, see each other's tears falling, see the passion of each other's heart, see each reflected in each other's eyes, all our joy and pain, all the fire raging round. She kisses me. 'How blest am I,' she whispers, 'in this discovering thee.' And let each other go, climb closer to John.

'Look,' he says, and shows us his scorched skin, the red of heat shining through the black of ash. Stretch out to touch him, try to soothe him. 'And look,' I say, drawing Lisa's hair back, showing how he's harmed her. Hold out her bandaged hands to him. 'So painful,' I say. 'So painful, John.' Tears run from his eyes, leave tracks on his cheeks, his chest. He doesn't move, doesn't speak as we clamber up to him. We hesitate. From the summit we see through the fierce air the yellow-helmeted firemen running to rescue us. All below us are the valley, the town, the city with its arched bridge far away. Behind are moors, going on as if for ever. We take John's hands, lead him, from the rocks onto the untouched heather on the other side. We begin to run towards the wilderness, tugging at our clothes.

THE
MARKET
STORIES

CONCENTRIC RINGS

THIS STORY IS NOT MINE. IT WAS TOLD TO ME BY ONE OF OUR many street performers, an acrobat who had specialised in spinning. Even in old age, at a time when he should be staggering towards death, or already lie rotting in his grave, he described intricate loops and spirals across the open areas of the city. They were astonishing performances, of an unnatural vigour, but they were also a deterioration, for it was said that in youth his spinning had been so rapid as to take him to the very edge of invisibility.

Though, whenever he passed by my desk in the bazaar, we called out polite greetings to each other, I had never spoken with him, and had come to believe that his reserve was the outcome of his contempt for my sedentary occupation. One morning, however, I looked up from my work to find him standing before me. He had lifted from the corner of my desk an object I had thrown there in frustration. He was fingering it, gazing at it as if at some reawakened memory.

I had found it the previous evening, in the course of clearing out my father's chests. It consisted of a pair of concentric rings, the inner leather ring being attached to a metal ring by a system of radiating springs. The inner ring was buckled, so that like a belt it could be expanded or contracted. My father had entered the long unconsciousness that was to precede his death, so he was unable to guide my understanding of it. I had cleaned it, oiled it, so that the buckle and springs had loosened, and it seemed to have regained its potential. But I could imagine no purpose for it. Was it a trap, the remains of some obscure engine or machine, an instrument of torture? The solutions which seemed most probable were an irritation, for I knew that I might accept as true a solution that bore no relation to the real truth. I had given up my private speculations, saw that they would have to be tested against the knowledge of someone else.

'Do you know what it is?' I asked.

'Of course. Though I thought it had been burned with the rest. Do you not know?'

'No.' I told him how I had come across it, and he laughed.

'Yes, he would want to keep some part of it,' he said, 'He was always sitting there, taking note. He missed nothing.'

'He's dying.'

'Yes, I heard. Still, I can see he's prepared you well.'

'He can't help me with this.'

'This? It'll tell you nothing about him.'

'I'm not interested in that. If you can tell me what it is, then just tell me.'

'It's not that easy.'

He looked about him. The bazaar was already filled with people, a potential audience.

'I should be working,' he said.

I invited him to sit in the chair beside me, where for years my father had sat, training me. He laughed again, and said I was truly my father's son, but then he shrugged, and sat there. For minutes, he was silent, ordering his memories, before he began.

'I'm an acrobat. I've always been one, like my father, like my father's father. It's my obsession and my life. I am that obsession, nothing more. I've spent all my energy on it, on becoming, and remaining, the finest acrobat, the greatest spinning man that this city's ever seen. I'm going to fail, of course. Better than anyone, I know how poor my performances are now, if I compare them with those of my youth. But what of it? Should I despair? No, even I, who try to oppose time, have to accept that we're all subject to it. Otherwise obsession would become madness, wouldn't it? I'm telling you this so that you'll understand that in order to become what I've become, I haven't been able to live like others do. For me, life is a constant training for performance. It's a constant spinning that only death will trip. The way I live cuts me off. It means that even though I live in a city packed with people, with people who watch me and applaud me, I can't live as they do. How can I? I see them, when they turn away after my performances, turn to a life of trivia, to a quest for futile pleasures, novelties. I'm not condemning them. I can even imagine the attractions of their lives, but I can't, because of my obsession, follow them. Anyway, because of all that, I've become a spectator, watching the life of a city that can't involve me. A poor spectator, certainly, because I've seen little to catch my attention even. But looking at these rings, I recall a time when an obsession as strong as my own gripped the lives of many. I watched the obsession grow, saw in it my own purpose of opposing time, of opposing death itself. Most intriguing of all, I watched an obsession that was shared, that contrasted vividly with my own isolation.'

He was silent again. I feared that the frustrations of sitting, of controlling words rather than movements would cause him to leave me. But he seemed to have forgotten his surroundings and his spectators, to be lost in himself, until the beginning of his story suddenly showed itself to him, and led him inexorably towards its end.

'How can I say it started? A woman came to the city. None of us knew who she was or where she came from. How could we? She spoke in grunts, like some animal. Some said they could hear patterns in her grunts that must have meaning, that she was speaking some language. If it was language, it wasn't one that even our most-travelled merchants had come across, and no one ever showed any sign of understanding it. Neither did she learn anything of ours. When we asked, 'Where did you come from?' and pointed inquiringly in several directions, she nodded vigorously, agreed that she came from all directions.

'I say she was a woman. And she was, I suppose, or the core of her was. But she was a woman changed into a beast of burden. The first time she was seen was when she came through the gates. She was tied between the shafts of a cart by ropes and belts that had cut deep sores into her flesh. She was leaning forward, almost on all fours. Sweat and blood from her wounds ran from her into the mud. When she got as far as the market place, she unloosened herself and fell down in a faint. Nobody went to help her. Some of the stall keepers inspected her cart – there were bundles of torn clothes, a few animal skins, boxes of bruised vegetables. They turned away in contempt. It seemed as if she was just one more of the inadequates who come here without possessions or gifts, to beg from us, or to sneak out of the shadows to grab satisfaction for their envies and their needs. She would have been left there, but when she recovered she started to unload her belongings, and arranged them like makeshift furniture, as if she was setting up home there. It enraged the stall keepers. They threw her things back into the cart, pushed her back between the shafts, told her to get out. She was like a nervous animal at first, dodging their blows, trembling, with a wild terror in her eyes. But that didn't last long. Her nervousness suddenly became rage and she fought back with a strength unseen in any other woman. It wasn't so much her strength that made them scatter, as the wild bestial howling with which she accompanied it – a sickening sound, evil, as if a demon was snarling from beneath her flesh.

'All this time I'd been working, but the noise had drawn away my spectators one by one, and I was left performing in front of a few drunkards. I went to see what was happening. By the time I arrived, and had slipped through to the front of the crowd, she had fixed up a ragged tent and was removing the last few boxes from the cart. Until she came to the last one, she threw them down carelessly, spilling their contents to the ground, but that last one she lifted as if it contained everything precious. She sat down cross-legged in the dirt, lifted a roll of sheepskin from the box, unrolled the sheepskin in her lap, and took out her child from it.

'Her child. I'd seen nothing like it. It was a boy, that's all we could be sure of, but the strangest boy I'd ever seen. He had a head as big as a man's, as big as ours are. Except for a few pale hairs for eyebrows it was completely hairless. His features were tiny, like tiny engravings on his skin, and his eyes, the palest, most watery blue eyes, were completely expressionless. That head seemed to be all of him that mattered. Beneath it was a body that was shrunken or had failed to grow. Usually, the body supports the head. In him, it was as if the body hung down from the head, was nothing but an attachment. He hardly had shoulders at all. The limbs were small and stunted, folded up as if they had never been used.

'Such an odd contrast they made, that pair. Such a child sitting on such a woman's lap. When she looked at us now, there was a trace of conquest in her eyes, and I remember thinking, when she lifted him to her breast and began to suckle him, how like a performer she seemed, knowing that she had stirred our interest, delighting in the knowledge that we were at once fascinated and repelled.

'I don't know. Maybe she was just a performer and nothing more. Maybe the whole thing was just a trick she had developed, a way of turning their handicaps into advantages, of gaining favour and charity wherever she went. Whatever it was, it was enough to turn part of this city mad.

'Early the next day, soon after dawn, I came up here as usual to practise before the crowds came. But what I saw, next to her tent, was enough to destroy any thought of work. The back of her cart was staked to the ground, so that the

98

shafts were tilted high. From one of the shafts hung a rope, and on the end of the rope, a noose about his neck, was the boy, turning slow circles in the breeze. I rushed towards him, yelling curses at his mother and at those who stood beneath him watching. I was about to leap up to him, to unfasten him, but someone held me back and said, '"Look. He's smiling."

'And he was. He was looking down and smiling.

'When I had recovered from my first surprise, and began to look closely at the boy, it seemed clear enough what was happening. Where his voice box should have been there was a pad of muscle, a continuation of the muscles at the sides and back of his neck. These muscles were so highly developed that they made an unbroken ring protecting his breathing passages. That, and the unnaturally light weight of his body, meant that the rope couldn't strangle him. As I say, it seemed clear enough, but you know what we're like here. Soon there were dozens of us standing there watching, and the most nonsensical theories about the boy's abilities began to be passed around – most of them based on the supposed supernatural powers of the boy, of his mother, or of both of them together. Anybody who put forward a more rational explanation was immediately ridiculed. Of course the confusion was helped by the fact that whenever the mother was encouraged to enter the debate, all she could contribute were her grunts.

'Like a good entertainer, she knew how to keep us there. All morning she kept lifting the boy out of his noose, showing him to us, allowing those who dared, to touch him, before tightening once more the rope around his neck. Each time she pushed him away from her a wave of horror and delight rushed through us. By afternoon, though, some people began to get bored with it – after all, it was just the same thing over and over. And people started to leave, either because of the boredom, or because they were tired of having their reasoning mocked. As the sun was going down she unfastened him for the last time, and began suckling him again, all the time murmuring gently into his ear. He kept lifting his head from her breast and looking at her. He made tiny mewing noises, like a small cat.

'I realised then that I'd gone a whole day without working. It made me angry, especially when I looked around and saw that I was one of the last few people left. Somehow we'd drawn closer and closer to the woman and her child, and we were crouched in a half-circle in front of them. I stood up quickly and went home. I must have been the last to leave, because next morning the others were still there, sleeping uncomfortably in the dirt.

'It was as if that first day had been a time for testing us out, for trimming down the audience to a core of true believers. Because after that she showed no interest in anyone except the ones who had stayed all night. She sat among them, passed the boy among them. At first they were just looking closely at him and inspecting him with their fingers, but pretty soon they began to nuzzle him, kiss him, press him close to their hearts. It was sickening, disgusting really, seeing how quickly grown people, men and women, had allowed themselves to be entranced by that grotesque pair. But we've seen a lot worse things here, and most of the rest of us just wanted to leave them to it and get on with our own lives. But that wasn't easy, because there they were, in the marketplace. They improved her tent for her, brought her food and clothing. They made the boy a manger, lined it with the finest and softest cloths. They brought their own bedding, set up their homes there. In all of this they seemed untouched by all the entreaties of their friends and families. The space became a strange encampment, right there in the city's heart.

'Though they were at the centre, it was as if they'd left the rest of us behind, as if they were going to something they'd waited their whole lives for. But what were they going to? An idiot mother and her idiot child. How do you explain something like that? It's like there's something missing from some people, isn't it? Most times they don't even know it. They just know they're discontented. They can't make their own lives be enough for them. There's a huge gap in them. They cover it over by working, by watching people like me, by seeking out novelties, by just continuing until they can't continue any more. Then they die, discontented as ever. But sometimes something happens, they see something, they hear something, something that makes them stop, makes them think about themselves and about what's missing. That should be a good thing, shouldn't it? It should show them how to change things, to make them better.

'It should. But it never happens like that. I've never seen it happen like that. It always goes wrong somehow; sometimes it's wrong right from the start. Sometimes the wrong something happens, or they see it wrongly, hear it wrongly, get the wrong meaning from it. So it's no wonder the changes they make are the wrong ones. Sometimes it doesn't matter too much – they just exchange one false life for another. But sometimes it does. I've seen people give up everything to follow a dream or an idea that they think will solve everything, but that can only lead them to their own destruction. It's a kind of madness, but that seems to be the only thing some people can find to fill up the gap in themselves – madness.

'That's what happened to those people. They turned mad, mad in what they said, and then mad in what they did. They said the woman and her son had been sent here. They didn't know where from and they didn't know who by. But it was deliberate that they didn't know, in the same way that it was deliberate that she didn't know how to speak to us. That way, the burden of understanding fell on us, and it was a burden, because it needed an effort of will, intelligence, imagination. Anybody who didn't make the effort would continue in their ignorance and cynicism.

'This is what their effort came to – they said that the woman and boy were rich with meaning. The woman, with her muscles and the marks left by years of strain, was a symbol of the body, something tied to the earth, doomed. Her boy was the outward image of the spirit, that in most of us lies dormant, unseen. When he was hanged, he showed that the spirit transcends the body and the earth, that it can defeat death itself.

'Of course there's no harm in talk like that. You can invent meanings for anything if you put your mind to it.

Some people spend their whole lives doing little else. But these people went further than that. They said that the boy's shape showed that the spirit is an embryo inside us, that it can be born in each of us as he was born from the body of his mother. In order that this could happen, they said that they did not have to abandon the body, that they did not have to die, but that their bodies must be reshaped so that they corresponded more exactly with the shape of the spirit as seen in the boy. In that way, the body and the spirit could be brought to live in harmony, as the mother and her child lived in harmony, that they could become a perfect pair. And in perfection, of course, there's no death. That was their final, and maddest belief – that they could become immortal.

'I keep saying they were mad. But wasn't it just as mad that a few people who believed something like that were surrounded every day by hundreds of other people who knew it was all nonsense, but who could do nothing to make them see that. Some of us did try, certainly, and even managed to persuade a few of them to see sense. The rest resisted everything. Their faith was like a huge wall that nobody would ever get over.

'And the rest of us, who were supposed to be the sane ones, but who did nothing to persuade anyone? I was typical. I knew it was nonsense, but somehow I managed to tell myself that it might not be, and most important of all, I wanted to see what would happen next.

'How do you change the body? It's not too difficult. It changes itself, adapts itself to the way you live. Mine's hard and muscular, because of the way I use it. Look at yours. It's already soft, a little flabby, because you're sitting most of the time, hardly using it at all. But these people wanted a most peculiar shape. They wanted most of their muscles to waste away, ideally to be like the boy's, so shrunken they couldn't even be used. At the same time, they wanted that thick pad of muscle around their throats. It was hardly a natural shape, so it called for a very unnatural discipline.

'These rings were just a fragment of that discipline, of a ludicrous apparatus and way of life that were designed to turn them into copies of the boy. Watch. The rings went over the head, like this, then the inside ring was tightened around the throat. They had chairs made. Above the seat, they could close the chairs around them in a tight tube. The outer metal ring was fixed over the top of the tube. Their legs were fastened to the bottom of the chair by straps. What it all meant was that the only part of the body that could be moved was the neck, and in order to move that, they had to pull against the pressure of the springs. So the whole contraption seemed perfect – it strengthened the neck, and weakened everything else.

'Of course it took a long time to get the chairs made, and it was expensive. Some of them had no trouble in affording it. Others sold their belongings, sometimes everything they owned. The ones who had nothing, neither money nor saleable possessions, tried to make do with imitations of the chair, but they ended up with nothing but awkward parodies of it. They were all in competition with each other. It was as if only the possession of a perfect chair allowed entry to the inner circle of the faithful. So the chair was another test –

those who failed it were no longer true believers. They tried to keep their attachment to the faith, but you could see that they were outcasts. Some of them became sickened by their position, and left the encampment altogether, tried to pick up the thread of their old lives again, but most of them stayed, and formed a dejected, rather pathetic group clinging to the fringes of the chair owners.

'At the centre, there were a dozen, who had kept their faith intact, and who had come into possession of a chair. They sat in a tight circle around the mother and her child. They had a brand new scaffold built, and twice each day, at sunrise and sunset, she stepped up to it with her boy in her arms, hanged him from it and pushed him away from herself, while the chair owners whimpered eerie melodies of praise. Though that ritual accentuated how far beyond our influence they had travelled, sometimes it seemed as if the whole city was feeding off them. Not only did we gain a perverse kind of entertainment from them, but a whole network of business and trade was formed around them. Though the boy had been seen to consume nothing but his mother's milk, they came to believe that their progress would be quickened if they ate only the meat of strong-necked beasts. Hearing this, hunters and merchants were forever adding to their heap of carcasses, and asking, and receiving, the most outrageous prices. And I don't think there was one apothecary at that time who didn't invent a cream, a pill or an ointment, and offer it to them as the perfect potion for shape-changing.

'They were employers, too. They hired large muscular men as a protection against the possible aggressions and supplications of heretical citizens. These bodyguards serviced the chair owners' needs. They fed them. They shaved them, at least twice each day, not just their faces but every part of them, so that they could imitate the perfect hairlessness of the boy. At regular intervals the bodyguards lifted them from their chairs, and carried them to latrines where they strained to force out the waste that might infect their purity.

'Living in such a way, it was hardly surprising that they made progress towards their ideal. They had to fit stronger and stronger springs about their necks, loosen the buckles to accommodate their growth. We saw when they were carried from the chairs how shrunken and wasted their other muscles became. Their skin was pale and slack, covered by sores and blemishes. Their faces when they passed by us were spectres, unfocused, staring bleakly at nothingness. Some said it was meditation. It wasn't. They were abandoned faces, drained of life.

'And as their lives drained, so did my germ of hope, of any faith I had somehow continued to imagine. It was finally destroyed when one of them awoke from his madness, tried to retreat from death.

'He had been a house builder in his past life, a vigorous, successful man. Even now you can see the results of his work in many of the city's streets. I don't know, perhaps an image from that past life, perhaps the face of some former friend or lover, found its way into his stillness and suddenly began to haunt him. Anyway, he began screaming – a wordless screaming filled with revulsion, terror. From somewhere he found the strength to fling open his chair as if to leap from it.

He fell from it, could hardly hold himself on all fours. He tried to squirm his way out from the circle but his every move was opposed by his own bodyguard, who finally lifted him, thrust him back into the chair. But again he flung open the chair and again fell from it. Several times the act was repeated, until the bodyguard lifted him high into the air and threw him out. Once they realised what was happening, the outcasts, whose progress to perfection, compared with that of the chair owners, had been so slow, began to release themselves from their own contraptions, and scrambled over each other, fighting to gain the vacant chair. Some bystanders, perhaps hoping that this first break in the circle might precipitate an end to the whole affair, rushed forward to restrain them, but they themselves were opposed with such violence by the bodyguards that they were forced to retreat. In the end the chair was again occupied, and the failed outcasts tied themselves up again, muttering their despair.

'We tried to help the one who had been thrown out, but at each touch he cowered, as if in fear of great pain. Broken, deformed and inarticulate, scorned even by those who had once loved him, he lay there for days, a beggar, feeding on the scraps and waste that were thrown at him, until one morning we found him dead.

'To the other chair owners that day, it was as if everything had happened in another world. It had, in a sense. It had happened in the world of the living, while they were entering the world of the dead. That's what it meant now. They had trained themselves into a stillness that wasn't calm or peace, but was a kind of stagnation, a rotting down. Like the rest of us, they had once had everything – a life of body, mind, spirit, but they had stopped using it, had refused to use it. And when life isn't used it just rots down into itself, as surely as the body rots into itself in the grave. That day life had tried to assert itself. It had demanded to be recognised, but it was too late. Even the creature it had asserted itself in was too far gone towards death to be able to do anything about it. Death had the upper hand. It squatted with that woman and that child at the centre of the ring of chairs, and inexorably sucked the owners of the chairs towards it. Already they existed in a kind of living death. At the most, there would perhaps be a few more bursts of violence. Then, soon enough, death would truly come into its own. They would die.

'I saw how mad it had been to hope that it might have ended in any other way. I gave myself completely to my work. I've been told that that was my best ever time. It's true. And it's true of many of the performers who were working then. We had a vigour that was almost desperate, that pressed us towards feats of greater and greater daring. Time and again we found the limits of our energies and skills, but even as we found them we found some means of going beyond them. It was because of the chair owners, of course. There they were, at our heart, and it was impossible to work without catching sight of them. They provoked us, they spun us on. How could we look at death without giving our almost miraculous display of death's opposite?

'Sometimes, because of the effect it had on our performances, I wish that it had lasted longer, that death had claimed them only after years of slow collapse. But it wasn't to be. The greatest work of my life was crammed into a few short weeks. Then the scaffolds were built, a ring of them, one at the back of each chair, a noose hanging down over the head of each owner. The scaffolds were to be the stage upon which they would give their finest performance. Their months of discipline, meditation, had all been directed towards it. The crowds came back, sat for a day waiting while the city was filled with the noise of hammering and sawing. And I joined them. Why were we there? Did we still hope that death could be cheated? Did we believe that the spirit had been caused to flourish in those mutilated bodies? In some faces there were the signs of such hope and faith, it's true. But the rest of us? We had been brought back as we can be brought back by any good entertainer's trick. We had the opportunity to be there at the end of a performance that had intrigued, inspired, bored and horrified us. We didn't want to miss the final flourish.

'The carpenters finished their work, walked away from it. Criticised by anyone, they merely shrugged. It was business, after all. Then there was silence for an hour, everything as normal.

'In the late afternoon, the bodyguards began to open the chairs, to loosen the straps and rings, to replace the rings with the ropes. As if only now understanding what had been so long prepared for, some of the crowd shrieked in protest, and leapt forward in a vain rescue attempt. They were thrown back at us, to begin a desperate sobbing, pierced by guilt.

'As usual, when the sun hung low over the walls, the woman lifted her boy and hanged him. He turned a few slow circles, and then, as if at some signal, though I saw none, each bodyguard gripped the free end of his rope and lifted his master from the chair.

'And that was the end of it all. The bodies gave a few last kicks against the madness. Some of them managed a strangled cry of anger or despair. But within a few minutes the only thing that moved them was the breeze, and the slow spinning of the ropes. At last, dead, they were able to give a reasonable imitation of the boy.'

At this, the acrobat stretched himself in his chair, arching his back, holding his arms high above his head. He yawned, and turned to me laughing.

'And that's what it had all been for,' he said, 'It's crazy, isn't it? Telling it all to you now, it's like telling a story. I can hardly believe that something like that really happened, and seemed to matter so much.'

'So they all died?' I asked.

'Of course. What else? They all died, and we stood watching, and did nothing.'

'What about the boy?'

'Oh, he was fine. Though he wouldn't have been if we could have got to him, nor would his mother, but as usual the bodyguards were in the way, and wouldn't let us near them. She started packing up straight away, put the boy in his box, tied herself to the cart, and set off. The bodyguards, who you could now see were probably more entranced than anyone, followed them. The outcasts went as well, limping, staggering and crawling – I doubt if they ever kept up.'

'Then you burned everything?'

'The whole lot. Except this, thanks to your father. We heaped everything up – chairs and scaffolds, the outcasts' contraptions, the meat and all the pills and potions. Then we threw the corpses themselves on top, and set light to it all. By the next morning nothing was left but a ring of smouldering ash.'

His story over, he was preparing to leave me, but I wanted to find a way to restrain him, and explore further a past that my father's unconsciousness denied me.

'And the way your work was stimulated then,' I said, 'Was there no other time that had a similar effect?'

But the question irritated him, and seemed to hurry his departure.

'How can I talk about that?' he said. 'With work like mine it's a matter of doing it, and talking isn't doing it. Anyway, good effects, bad effects – you take them as they come.'

He had withdrawn from me. He shook my hand and left, walking stealthily towards the centre of the bazaar. I tried to return to my own work, but the commissioned letters, the bills of sale and the announcements remained unwritten. Soon I put down my pen and followed him, stood in the crowd that watched him, cheered his skill, gasped at his daring, applauded his deteriorating spinning towards death.

Dark Cube

He was a familiar figure in the bazaar, yet he was known to no one. Each morning from the stalls he bought the simple requirements of life, held conversation with no one, took no interest in our attractions and entertainments, and returned in silence, looking neither to left nor right, to the warren of alleys and passages from which he had come. Greeted by others, he merely dipped his head lower, quickened his step.

Ever eager to speculate and imagine, some said that he must surely be involved in some obscure experimentation or research, to be so unmoved by the life and society of his city. Others scorned this. His aspect of seriousness and deep meditation, they said, was in truth the mask worn by an extreme emptiness and stupidity. He did not react because he had nothing with which to react. Yet others pitied him, saying that he had turned his face from his contemporaries in order to search the darkness in himself, only to find himself entangled in the alleyways that would entangle us all, were it not for our grateful participation in our time. Whatever our view, we all agreed that he had little to offer our time, and we learned to tolerate, and to ignore, his voluntary isolation.

The first time that he stayed with us, therefore, it was the fact of his staying, and the fact of his wanting to perform for us, which amazed us, rather than the performance itself, which seemed absurd.

It was evening. Released from the day's burdens, we had come together to be amused, refreshed and entertained. The sun had sunk over the palace, and on the stalls hundreds of tiny, differently coloured lamps were being lit.

Holding before him a small cubical wooden casket from whose joints a light gleamed, he appeared in the space among some tables, and called for those who dined there to attend him. To each group in turn he showed the box, and then to the other intrigued groups who soon came to stand about him, nudging each other and winking their amusement.

It was a bare, unornamented, hinged box. He lifted the lid, and lowered it so that it hung down against one of the sides. Then he released each side and they fell down to hang over his hand, leaving the whole interior of the box exposed. In that interior, supported by the base, was a single candle whose flame flickered uneasily above his trembling arm, and which swayed back and forth as he turned to exhibit it to each section of his audience. All leaned closer, certain that they had been brought together to see more in the box than a single candle and its flame. But they had not. He extinguished the flame, closed the box, moved from the centre of the crowd, and attempted to force his way through the knotted ring of bodies. But of course they resisted him, and started to mock him. Is that all there is? they called. Do you expect to satisfy us with that?

He raised his arm, hushing them.

'See how in darkness,' he said, 'we see the light.'

And with us torn by hilarity, he was able to leave us, with

our proven knowledge that he was a fool.

Next day he returned to find that his performance had caused him to become the centre of attention. Encouraged by their parents, children trailed him as he came out from the alleyways, forming a procession loud with their squealed music and mock praise. Dogs leapt and tore at his cloak. Stall keepers and purchasers hailed him, demanded more demonstrations of his spectacular skills and learning.

'Bring out your box,' they called, 'Bring out your box.'

Reaching an open space, he turned to his followers, and from a deep pocket did bring out the box. The crowd gasped, imitating awe.

The performance was repeated. The box was exhibited and opened. But this time, as he released the sides, we saw that there was no candle, and to our delight, someone shouted,

'See how in light, we see the darkness.'

When all sides were released, there appeared to be another box, until now enclosed within the first. It was perfectly black, with no reflection on its surface, without joints or hinges. He turned, showing it, and we demanded that he open it.

In answer, he went to the stall of a seller of caged birds, and with his free hand brought out the most dazzlingly coloured bird from its cage. Muttering to it, he allowed it to perch for a moment on his finger, singing, before, without opening hinges or loosening joints, he placed the bird inside the box, so that we could see nothing of it, but could hear its continuing sweet song. Silent, we edged in circles around him, leaning close, searching for an opening, a glimpse of the lost bird. But it only appeared when he struck the wooden base, and it dashed out, flying wildly to the sky.

This time, as he closed the box, and replaced it among the folds of his heavy garments, we moved aside, allowing him to leave us, and the procession that followed him was hushed, confused. Though at the edge of the bazaar we called after him, 'What is it? Explain it. Let us inspect it,' he continued in his accustomed way, looking neither to left nor right, his head hung low. And those who trailed him further, and peered through his window and the frame of his door, returned that evening without tales of laboratories, practised illusion or sorcery, but told of him sitting in a dark room, meditating, with the box open before him, and his hands lost in the blackness within.

In the weeks that followed, he dispelled all our ignorance. He came back regularly, and showed us all there was to show. We saw that the interior of the wooden box was not another box, but was a perfect cube of darkness that obscured anything that entered it, and that no light could dispel. It was a darkness deeper than the darkness of night, for in it candles went on burning, without emitting rays. He beckoned us close to it, and copying him we learned the courage to place our hands there and see them lost even while we could feel them and clench them and know that they were there, until after a time courage was no longer needed and the dark cube became our plaything. We dipped our cheeks and chins in it, making laughably severed heads, or went lower and stared into a darkness that had no visible exit, yet just beyond which were the faces of our grinning friends.

But as with all playthings, boredom was its burden, and again we began to ask, is this all there is? Though he encouraged none of it, and resisted all questioning, we argued among ourselves, many claiming to have divined the true nature and power of his darkness. The lame and the withered were brought, to rest their limbs in it, searching for healing. Mothers bathed their children in it, as if in some ritual cleansing or benediction. Groups of acolytes formed, who took no part in our play, but at the opening of the box bowed their heads and chanted low murmurous sounds of confession and praise. Others turned away, and warned that an object so negative could only cause dismay and suffering around itself.

Yet the city thrived, as always, and was beset by neither increased blessings nor calamities. The lame continued limping. The withered withered. Children grew as they were due to grow, straight or stilted, luminous or dull. So that finally even those who had imagined its unearthly goodness or malevolence were brought to recognise: the darkness had no power, only its quality of being dark. It was indeed all there was.

Fascination, and his audiences, waned. We shrugged him back to his barren meditations, and he became again the solitary, bowed figure, hurrying out from and into his alleyways, with nothing to communicate or to perform, until one day we realised he was no longer even that. Unseen, he was forgotten, lost in the obscurity of the past.

Only once, years later, were we reminded of him. A group of entertainers erected before us a tall wooden casket on a stage. Opening it, they revealed the masked, heavily cloaked figure of a man. They pulled away the masks and cloaks, and left an unclothed darkness, through which they passed their hands and in which they stood, calling to us. But we were unimpressed. It was an old illusion, by then we had been seduced by other wonders, and darkness in the shape of man was unable to amaze us.

THE SNAKE CHARMER

IN ORDER THAT HE MIGHT WORK WITH TRUTH RATHER THAN WITH illusion, and charm snakes whose venom had not been milked from them, he led a solitary childhood of abstinence and meditation. Only when the snakes were subject to his will, when his body was trained and his spirit disciplined, did he begin to practise his craft before the farmworkers and artisans of isolated villages. Though the rewards of this were small, they were sufficient to satisfy his worldly needs, and he showed no desire to perform before more sophisticated or larger audiences. However, news of his prowess spread throughout the country. Truth mingled with rumour and speculation. It was said that all living things, not only snakes, were entranced by his movements, his music and his unwavering gaze. When he played his pipes, plants leaned towards him, the fierce became tame. And in his music men heard the elusive rhythms of their souls.

It was also said that his snakes were capable of terrible vengeance – provoked by lack of faith, immediately they struck the disbeliever, in this way bringing both proof and inevitable death.

Hearing of him, we sent messengers, asking that he should come to the city, and give evidence of the reality behind these strange reports. On his arrival, because of his awkwardness before us, the way he could never meet another person's eye, or arrange his words as sense, we took him to be only another crazed or fraudulent sorcerer, quickly to be despatched into obscurity. Yet when he began to play, and the snakes to uncoil from their baskets, all vestiges of shyness left him, and our scepticism was destroyed.

Remaining untouched by all the temptations of luxury and fame which were now held up before him, he asked only for food and simple lodging, and we found him rooms close to the thick walls that surround the palace at the centre. Outside the walls we built a stage, elevated so that all members of his growing audiences might easily see him, to wonder at his artistry and at the things they believed he made them see inside themselves. Upon his stage, among so many watchers, many of whom had travelled across distant frontiers and dangerous seas in order to be there, he remained in isolation. Unknown, he was honoured yet feared by all of us.

There were also those, even within the city itself, for whom he remained not only unknown but unseen. These were the veiled daughters of the governors, who spend their days hidden deep within the palace, protected, confined to exotic rooms and tiny walled courtyards. For them, the snake charmer played his pipes beyond unknown corridors, unopened doors. But even to them, in their expectant and passionate obscurity, the rumours came, and they desired to see.

Only one of them succeeded. His attraction awakened in her the courage to bribe and to deceive, to recognise the form and power of her own enchantment, impelled her to break her bounds. One morning she appeared on the battlements, and stared down to the crowd, searching out the swaying body of the snake charmer. As she pulled away her disguises and lowered her veil, movements and murmurings afflicted the audience, and the snake charmer was aware of being no longer the centre of all attention. Beyond his snakes, the eyes turned towards something more elevated and surprising than he. And he turned, wishing only to catch a glimpse of this unique something, but her gaze, and the sudden uncoiling of the darkness in himself, caused him to stare.

Now the snakes struck, and the crowd fled from their ungoverned violence. On the battlements, as the body tumbled from the stage below, guards stepped forward, covering the girl, and hurrying her into the disillusioned frantic centre of the palace.

THE EYE OF GOD

HE WENT JOYFULLY WHEN WE TURNED HIM OUT, FOR HE BELIEVED IN words, not only the words with which he had pestered us for so long, but those with which we deceived him. When he spoke of a god who had abandoned us, he meant a god who had truly abandoned us, who had removed himself from us, and who might be discovered again, somewhere beyond the city walls. And when we, bored by his pestering, said that we too had come to believe in that god, and to repent our sins, he believed that we truly believed and truly repented.

Of course, he began to call out his thanks and praise.

'Finally they listen to your words, of which I am the instrument. Finally their eyes are cleared, and they see the path to righteousness. Truth has entered our city. Your city returns to you.'

'And yet,' we asked, 'Who do you call to? Your words that rend the air, here between the walls, who can hear them? Though we will change, and change the city, how can God come to know of that change, unless there is one among us courageous and virtuous enough to discover God once more, and take the message of our change to God?'

With that, we were rid of him. It was he who went out, searching, a messenger bearing our promises, to begin, we supposed, a life of wretched solitary wandering. He left nothing but a memory which, as those who remembered him died, itself began to die.

Years later, when he returned so changed, shrunken, his bones protruding through scaly torn skin, his eyes bulging in their sockets, even those of us capable of remembering him did not know him. Lamenting, cursing, he seemed only another of the furious and deluded prophets who come regularly through the city gates, and whom we cast out or ignore. It was only when he began to call us by name, to remind us of our promises, and to demand to know, had we, who had burdened him with his quest, fallen so far that we took no interest in the discoveries of that quest, that we attended to him.

He had returned to mould God for us in the stones and dust of the streets. He knelt among us and traced the outline of the city, its two concentric walls, in the dirt. This, he told us, was the eye of God. He traced another outline of another city, which was the other eye of God. Between his cities he placed stones, representing the mountains that were the nose and brow of God, and there were caverns in these mountains, entering the mouth of God.

He had discovered a god who lies supine, who is the earth itself, washed by seas which are his tears, shed for the corruption of those who populate his skin. Upon this god, we inhabit the colouring of the eye. Outside us is the countryside of cornea, lid and cheek. Within us, behind our inner wall, from the pupil of his city, God stares.

Someone sniggered.

'Can you not see it?' he demanded. 'Can you not see?'

We who knew him, though we became skilful in avoiding him, had learned pity, and we did not scorn or shun him. Finding him before us, we would listen patiently, make polite, accommodating noises.

'Yes indeed,' we would say. 'Truly a remarkable discovery. We will strive to live well.'

But he began to turn from us, and to speak only to those who sought him and questioned him and gathered ever more eagerly to their sport. From my desk in the bazaar I would watch them, and hear how little he, and we of the city, had changed. Soon his questioners had led him to the beginning of another, and more perilous, quest.

'Master,' they said, 'if the city is God's eye, then does God see us?'

'He does not want to see us. He stares at the wonder of his day and the glory of his night. He feels us, though, as we would feel a thousand grains of dust in our eye. Imagine such an agony.'

'Yet when I feel dust in my eye, I search it out. I rub, sniff, blow until I am rid of it. Is God unable to do this?'

'God loves his people, and though he lies stunned by the pain they cause him, he will not harm them. He comforts himself with the contemplation of his universe, and he has caused walls to be built, which protect him from the vision of our desolation.'

'But what of those inside the walls?'

'They are God's true people. They know him and praise him. They receive his benefits and walk forever in his sight.

They, too, know how far we outside have fallen, and they detest us for it.'

'But you also know him.'

'Some must carry that burden, knowing God and knowing that few will listen to their words. In death, God will know me and receive me.'

'But see how we listen. We also have come to know God.'

'Then live righteously, and God will receive you also.'

'But Master, is it right that so many of us here, having listened to you, know God and wish to alleviate his pain, and yet because of his walls and his stupefaction he is unable to realise that his people are at last turning to him in the desire to know his will? Is it right to allow God to imagine an agony that is already fading?'

At this point, wishing to restrain him, I stepped forward, and tried to take part in the questioning.

'Tell me, Master,' I said. 'This other city, is it a city like ours? Are people there as fallen as we are here?'

But he would not hear me. He stared back at his oppressors, finally recognising the true burden of his faith.

'Can it be,' he said, 'that having been the messenger of God among his people, I must again become the messenger of the people to their god? And since I have come to know God, must God now come to know me?'

Amid the assent of the others, I shouted,

'Can you not see how they beguile you, as you were beguiled by others in the past? Can you not see how they laugh, provoking you, and urge you to suffer for their amusement?'

But he was far gone in his madness. He spat at me, saying,

'You who sent out lies to God, who continue to see lies when truth is before you, who live on God but pay no heed to him, you are the beguiled, and yours will be the suffering. God will know his own, and he will also know you.'

'Master,' said one of them, taking his arm and turning him from me, 'What will you do?'

That evening, he stood before the huge door that is set into the walls that surround the palace, calling for it to be opened.

'I come to God with a message from his people,' he shouted.

But no matter how violently he beat upon the door, nor how loud his voice, there came no answer, and those who had come to watch his humiliation began to drift away, disappointed. Only a few were left when at last a small hatch in the door slid open, framing a grinning face that spat curses and saliva at him, and quickly slid shut again.

Again I went to him and tried to comfort him.

'Come away,' I said. 'Only harm can come from this. Do not doubt that God knows you, and wishes you to work among his people.'

But others, dissatisfied, pressed past me.

'Your reception is no surprise to us, Master,' they said. 'How can we expect a god's protectors to see with the discernment of a god? You must avoid them, go directly to his sight.'

As they led him away, I grabbed one of them angrily.

'Be content,' I said. 'Press him no further.'

'Press him? We show him his desires, no more.'
'He will die for them.'
'Perhaps. Or bring us truth.'
'You cannot believe that.'
'Can't I? And you — what do you believe?'

Night fell. Stars stretched from wall to wall. A huge moon rose over the rooftops. He sat silently in the dust, his back to the wall, flanked by guardians, staring to where God stared. They brought him ladders, and ropes with hooks attached to them.

'Master,' they said, 'Everything is prepared.'

He thanked them and we withdrew to the shadows, watching, as he draped a rope across his shoulders, leaned the longest ladder against the wall, and began to climb. At the top of the ladder, invigorated by his faith, he swung the rope time after time until it caught fast in the battlements, and he was able to drag himself from our sight.

For a time we waited, listening, but there were only the familiar sounds of the city, and the thickening night.

I went to my bed, but sleep refused me, so all night, below the glistening sky, I shuffled through the alleyways, through the stench of waste, the noise of children whining, beggars snoring, the snuffling of diseased dogs. At dawn I went gratefully to my desk in the bazaar, and while the commotion around me grew, lost myself in the copying of bills of sale, letters of recommendation, notifications of births, entertainments and deaths. Then I must have slept, for when they roused me my head was resting on my papers, that were soaked with sweat.

He had been found lying by the wall. Already a crowd had gathered, who groaned in sympathy with his pain, and some had taken upon themselves the task of tending with splints and bandages his broken limbs and torn skin. But even now there were tormentors. What had he seen? they asked. Had God not received him, not recognised him? He stared back towards them through bleeding eyes. I forced my way to him, and began to clean his eyes, that beneath the blood were pierced, sunken and sightless. While we worked he groaned, whether in agony or gratitude we could not tell, so that we feared his tongue had been cut out also, but forcing open his mouth, we found it curled tightly back, clenched against his palate.

When we had finished, though we had little hope that he might live, we lifted him onto a handcart and took him to the shadows beneath the awnings of the bazaar, and pressed cloths soaked with water to his lips. He submitted in silence to all we did for him.

Soon, those who had followed us were drawn by other tasks and interests. They had to push past us, until the stallholders began to rebuke us, to say that surely a more decent place could be found for a dying man. And we who had cared for him, and who I now realised were of the same generation, glanced at each other with bitter understanding.

It was I who took him in. We lifted him from the cart, carried him through the twisting stairways to my room, laid him across my bed. He inhabits it still. I tend his wounds, share food with him, and sleep curled in the angle of the walls.

Each day I wake in the hope of not hearing his breathing. Often visitors come, wanting to question him, or merely to see him, but I refuse them entry. There would be no purpose to it. Day and night he lies, silent and hideously wide-eyed, bearing his knowledge and his pain.

SPOTLIGHT

IT STARTED AS A GAME, IN OCTOBER, ON THE NIGHT THE CLOCKS WENT back. As usual, Anthony was playing on the green. As usual, I was watching from the window. There were simple games, ball games, skipping games. Girls were singing and chanting and their voices echoed from the houses all around. As it darkened, I watched them all huddle together, then I watched Anthony come back to the house. He wanted a torch, he said. It was for a new game. A game played in the dark.

'What game?' I whispered.

He sighed.

'Oh, mother,' he said. 'It's called Spotlight.'

He stood there with his hand on his hip.

'Please,' he said. 'They're waiting for me, mother. Give me the torch and let me go.'

I held my breath. I held his arm. I peered out into the dusk, saw the white expectant faces of his friends beyond the garden wall.

Stay inside, I wanted to say, but I couldn't speak. I saw Robert watching me, assessing me.

'Please,' said Anthony. 'You're hurting me.'

It was Robert who found the torch, Robert who released Anthony, Robert who sent him out and then turned to me, sighing, and held me tight.

David Almond

'You have to stop clinging to him,' he told me. 'You have to stop scaring him.'

'I know. But I didn't stop him, did I?' I pointed to the children heading out into the dark. 'Look, I let him go.'

Spotlight. It became the only game for night. Each dusk that autumn the children gathered at the centre of the green, around the monument that was their bay. They stood impatient, glancing up towards the sky, the multiplying stars. In someone's hand the torch flashed on and off, on and off. Each night they began early, when the day's light hadn't entirely left the sky, and rushed out towards the alleyways, garden walls and hedges at the limits of the green. Once they had settled and the squealing of the youngest ones had stopped, the only sound came from the one child left at the centre, who bent low with his head held in his hands, filling the air with the loud drone of his counting: 'One... two... three... four...' Until at last with a cry of 'Coming out!' he switched on the torch, left the centre, began a long search punctuated by wild screams of discovery, sudden struggles, frantic races to the bay.

Each night I watched from the window. I saw the white plumes of their breath, heard the high-pitched excited voices, the fearful laughter. I saw how the game dispersed and grew, and I knew how Anthony deceived me. Despite our agreement that the game should never go beyond the hedgerow at the limits of the green, that quickly became too tame for all of them. Each night I saw the torch beam flashing further into the wilderness outside. And in the daytime, when we walked

130

out there, where all the ancient pits and shafts had been, we saw how the ground was becoming riddled with hiding places, how the turf could be lifted in blanket-sized sections to expose the ancient ash and the impressions of children's bodies beneath.

Robert told me, 'It's helping him to settle here. And you have to allow him secrecy. It's part of growing. He's fine. Everything's fine.'

I told myself that he was right. It was just a game. There was nothing to fear. But when with the other parents I began to shout my child's name time after time into the dark, I never truly expected him to come back. But come he did, an age after I'd begun, with his clothes filthy, his hands and face scraped by twigs and thorns and grit, and with his eyes abstracted and wide, as if I'd called him back from an adventure, or from some astounding dream...

My own dream, of coming here, had formed a year back, when we lived in the city, that nightmare place. Garish noise and light by day, perilous dark at night. All around us were ruined streets. I saw needles and glue tubes, drained cans of lighter fluid scattered in gardens and gutters. In the shadows I saw beasts of men with bottles in their fists and slurred curses on their tongues. Damaged children huddled in doorways, slept in half-demolished houses. We lived behind locked doors, shuttered windows. We defended ourselves with fences and alarms and lights. I kept Anthony inside. I never let him go out alone into the dark. Robert told me I was stifling the boy. I must begin to let him go. I pointed from the window. Can you not see them waiting for him? I demanded.

There, look. There and there and there. Constantly, Robert tried to soothe me. It was not so bad as I imagined, he told me: I saw only the dark things, only the bad. He persuaded me to go to doctors who fed me tablets, recommended yoga classes, relaxation classes. They talked of an imbalance in my nature, that caused me to see my surroundings as vindictive. They suggested that perhaps another child... Another child? They saw nothing. How could we bring up another child there?

I saw further than all of them. I saw all the dangers. I saw into the city's dreadful heart, and then one sunlit afternoon, when I raised my eyes, I saw the gentle surroundings that might give us an escape. Beyond and above the city were the moors rising to the sky. So green, so calm, surrounded by such gentle light. That's where we should go, I said to Robert. To that green and peaceful place. We can raise our child there. We can give him his freedom there.

He held me tight.

Will it be better there? he asked.

Yes. Oh, yes.

We got out. We sold the house and came up into this lovely place. Here were small villages nestling on hillsides, green paddocks and hawthorn hedges, clean air and space and light. A revitalised place. A place that had been scarred for centuries was becoming pastoral again. We had more than half a year of contentment here: the spring given to restoring our new home, then the long summer of our own renewal, each day seeming further to disentangle us from the city and our past. Anthony threw off his memories and plunged into the freedom offered by this place, by all his new friends. I felt my own nightmares dispersing slowly, I felt something like joy entering my heart.

'It's healed us all,' Robert would say, as we watched from our window the children playing in the sun. 'We should have left years ago...'

We prepared early for winter, hoarding food and fuel. During our walks, we'd glance up towards the high Pennine horizon, anticipating storms. But late autumn, the first weeks of winter, seemed paradoxically to pass by in intensifying light: icy days without a breath of wind, the sun blazing low over the horizon, the dawns mauve, the twilights amber, burning into nights that sparkled with frost and stars. We lit our Christmas lights and for the first time understood that this festival truly was the celebration of life's flame burning in the dark.

I watched the colours dance across Anthony's eyes, and I told him, 'You'll be so happy here. You couldn't have a better place to grow...'

On Midwinter's eve we gathered bright holly from the hedges. Walking back, we stopped at the centre of the green; Robert took Anthony's hand and pressed it to the monument's cold stone. He traced the date of the pit disaster, the column of names worn smooth by a century and a half of northern weather.

'Just think,' he said. 'Children on all fours in the dark. Crawling, never seeing daylight. If we'd lived then...'

I pulled their hands away.

'All that's over now. This place is peaceful countryside again. There's no more going down into the dark...'

But he continued, told us how they'd landscaped the pit heaps, blocked up the shafts. He said there were workings down there cut off since the disaster. He shrugged off my restraining hand. He smiled, so comforting.

'He has to learn these things,' he said. 'These things have to be remembered.'

'You're frightening him,' I said, but trembling out there on the ancient turf, I knew it was I who was scared, who gripped Anthony's hand tight until he told me,

'You're hurting, mother. Let me go.'

That night I was woken by his screams. I went to his bed and his eyes were wild in the light from the bedside lamp.

'They're digging further down,' he gasped.

He gripped me harder than he ever had.

'They're getting down to where the bones are!'

It took an age, but I thought I'd calmed him. I thought he was sleeping, and I was leaving him.

'Who's that in the light?' he yelled.

Next day, Midwinter's Day, at dusk, I held him back as he prepared to go out to the green.

'Anthony,' I whispered. 'Not tonight.'

'Oh, mother!' he said, and I heard in his voice how tedious I could be to him.

He stepped out with the torch in his hand.

'It was only a dream,' he muttered. 'It's just a game...'

I watched through the window. I peered out through

the tunnel of my hands. I saw the familiar gathering and dispersal, watched the lone crouched figure at the monument, and this time it was Anthony, his voice counting. He counted backwards, down to one and 'Coming out!' He stood erect, and switched on the torch, which suddenly deepened the darkness all around. Then he headed out towards the waste. For minutes there was only the beam lifting and falling through the tangled hedge and someone out there screaming.

Robert called me from the fireside: 'What you doing? Come and drink something. Come and sit with me. Leave the boy alone.'

The torchlight moved further out, was a thin beam moving vertically across the earth.

'Anthony,' I whispered. 'Come back in.'

I went out through the back door, began to move across the green. Once more, someone was screaming. I heard Anthony coming back, heard him ripping the hedge in his need to break through. Then he ran with the light dancing furiously in his fist and a shadowed figure running at his heels. He was first to bay, and he retched, gasped, gathered his breath to go out again.

I stifled my cry but the beam swung to me and caught me.

'Who's that?' he said: a deep whisper, menacing, amused. Then came his bitter, 'What you doing out?'

'Where's the one who chased you?' I asked him. I ran, grabbed the torch, swung it in a circle around us: no one at the monument, no one on the green. 'Where is he? Where?' I put my arm around him, tried to hold him. 'What did you find out there?'

He shoved me off. In the glare of the torchlight I saw the rage he felt for me.

'What did you find out there? What was chasing you?'

'Oh, mother,' he said, and then he left, cursing me, racing back into the night.

I stared back at the houses, their windows filled with hundreds of tiny lights. I cried, leaning on the ice-cold stone, and I switched the torch off and on, off and on. The wide circle around the monument remained deserted. Then I followed him. I crossed the green, crawled on all fours through the tangles of the hedge. Outside, in deeper darkness and on broken ground, I walked awkwardly, clumsily. All around me were shifting shadows, children sniggering. I crouched, shone my torch into the hollows, found nothing. I lifted the blankets of turf, and beneath them, in the light, caught nothing. I moved further out, and all the time I whispered, 'Anthony! Anthony!' There were more hedges to push through, more pits to trip me. Soon the sniggering and the shifting stopped. The earth became more meagre. I felt the loose ash beneath my feet, tussocks of turf that had never taken. The village was tiny, a cluster of stars against the black. I'd come too far. 'Anthony,' I whispered. 'Oh, Anthony.' And at last, from miles away, from right back where I'd started, came his own cry: 'Mother! Mother!' I turned quickly, tripped, fell flat against the earth. My palms were scored by the grit, I tasted blood on my lips. I cursed myself, reached out for the torch, and all around me the earth began to open, and they began to come out from their hollows and hiding places. Children, dozens of them, half-naked, pushing away the turf and grit with skinny hands, then coming at me with their scent of firedamp and death and their whispering, 'Who's this? Who's this? Who's this?'

AFTER THE
ABANDONED
WHARVES

AFTER THE ABANDONED WHARVES, THE DEMOLISHED WAREHOUSES, the streets of already-deserted homes, John skirted the high fences of the Marina, crossed the waste land, came to the entrance to Balmoral, where he shuddered, came to a halt, stood dead still in the silence, the early morning heat. Balmoral. This place. This hell. Why did they make him enter here, morning after morning...?

Deep cul-de-sacs, rings of pebbledash houses with desolate greens at their hearts. At the entrance, sprayed massively in red across the road: NO. BALMORAL SAYS NO. The worst streets, always the worst streets, for all the years he'd been coming here. Every other letter a final demand or a summons. Hardly a window left, plywood where the glass should be. Streetlights that had failed years back. Two-year-olds in nothing but scruffy vests running round in packs. The Armstrongs and the Askews and the Gladstones, screwing round at will, so the whole place had turned to one big crazy clan with the craziness getting worse at every breeding. Where for every kid hauled out and into care another two were born. Two more savages. Two more little beasts. Like their dogs, these people. Wild, and getting wilder. Dogs. The big brown bugger in 36, massive snout and a mane like a lion, that you never heard coming, knew nothing of till it was at your back with its gob snapping and snarling. The ones that waited behind the door till you were shoving the letters through, then went on like they were coming out the flap at you, tongues and teeth rammed up and howling at the opening. Alsatians raging at the windows as you entered the garden. Dobermans that even the owners were terrified of, keeping them half-choked with steel chains and building cages – bloody cages – in the gardens for them. Ten stone Rottweilers that'd eat your own kids if you turned your back on them. They called them defenders. They said they needed them. They called them guardians, protectors, pets. He shuddered again. He'd heard the talk of worse, devil dogs or dragon dogs or something coming from the States. One of the guys had sworn he'd already seen one on his rounds. Teeth like blades, he'd said. Killer's eyes. Chained to a clothes post like a bloody bear. And when it saw you, and started thrashing and howling, like something straight out of a nightmare, heading straight from hell...

He stood there, staring in. How'd it come to this? How'd they let it come to this? He'd seen it way back, years back. There's trouble comin, he'd said. There's bother festerin in there. But they'd done nothing, gone on doing nothing, and the more they'd done nothing the more the whole place'd turned to jungle, crazy people and wild dogs all shacked up together, feeding off each other, whipping up each other... And now they'd tried to shift them and found it was too late, the wildness ran too deep. They wouldn't shift...

They'd been on TV, grunting about their rights and their intentions. They stood there in a semi-circle at the entrance and you could see the effort it took to civilise themselves. You could see the clenched fists, hear them gulping back the curses and the screams. What's this Marina to the likes of us? they asked. Why should we move for it? Where would we go? To hell, whispered John, squatting on the floor beside the screen, pointing to individual faces. That one, he said. And that one, look. They're the ones, love. Knife you quick as look at you. Animals, he said. You don't know the half of it, love.

Alison leaned over, touched him on the shoulder.

But look at the children, she whispered.

He looked. Unkempt things with mocking faces. Half-human things. He knew them, he'd seen them.

Angels, she whispered. Little innocents.

John laughed. Innocents!

Oh, love, she whispered, and she knelt by him.

We could take one, she said. Foster one. We could love one, John. Look at that one, that pretty one.

But look closely, love. There'll be paws where her hands an feet should be. There'll be hair runnin down the spine.

Oh, John.

It's true. Look at the fathers. Look at the eyes on them. Look at the sluts of mothers.

Oh, John...

We should brick them up. They'd soon be at each other's throats...

She pushed him away.

Just a matter then of sendin the bulldozers in, turnin them over into the rubble. Kids, dogs, whole soddin lot of them...

Stop it, she told him. Stop it...!

Nothing moved. Dust from the sites had settled on the roofs, in the gutters, in the uneven joints between the paving stones. It had settled on the house walls themselves, amongst the tiny pebbles, making them paler, bleaker things. The gardens were bleached and cracked by this summer's endless heat. Through the gaps between the houses he saw the river glistening, the cranes, the long-promised wonderful constructions: apartments and offices that would look down upon new plazas and new quays, upon bright sails dancing in the breeze. Everywhere the billboards showed how things would be, how this place would wake up soon into its brighter morning... The Marina. He grinned. Get it built. Get it over with. At least they won't bring devil dogs to the Marina. At least they won't end up screwing their own kids in the Marina...

A bony labrador moved out onto the road. It lay there sluggish, head resting on its paws, and even from this distance he saw the pink tongue hanging down, heard the panting. He shuddered again. He opened his sack, looked in. Bills, circulars, Readers' Digest nonsense, garish promises of excitement and wealth. He scanned the houses, saw no one but a little girl perched on a front step, and no one but she and the dog watched as he turned and walked away. So what? He'd known men take whole deliveries home, do their own personal sorting over a bacon sandwich and a cup of tea. Nobody had come to harm. Nobody had noticed anything had been missed. The man had a morning off, the good mail got delivered next morning sharp. Nobody but the postman had to bother with the junk... He'd tried it once, wandered in on her one dark February morning with his bag stuffed full and a grin on his face. Much good that had done him, the way she'd gone at him. Decency. Honesty. Caring for your fellow man. You know I'm right. John, you know I'm right. You don't know these people, he'd replied. You don't know what beasts they are. If you saw...

That had been an age before the Marina nonsense, an age before their own nonsense. These days when he walked away he ditched Balmoral's mail in skips and half-demolished buildings. He slung it out into the river in stone-weighted carrier bags. Then he'd wander through the sites, peer at the billboards, watch the future taking shape. Later, at home, he'd catch her staring.

Are you all right, John? she'd keep asking. Are you all right...?

His route led him to the waste land behind Balmoral, where the burned-out cars were, where the kids had dug deep trenches, covered them over with nicked corrugated steel so they could sniff and snort and screw in peace. He watched for dogs coming at him from the trenches or behind the cars. He picked up a snapped-off car aerial, ready to protect himself. But there were none nearby, only some mongrel a hundred yards away, engrossed in butting something dark and bloody in the earth, tearing at it with its teeth...

'Mister... mister!'

The little girl, in long grass, the dog at her side. She stood with her arm around its neck, her face level with its jaws, and her eyes were filled with fright.

'Please, Mister!'

He didn't move. Little blonde thing, maybe six years old, her frock pink and filthy, her hair knotted and wild. He imagined Alison, how she would reach down to such a child, touch shoulders, cheeks, hair, murmuring of loveliness, how she'd come to him later, whispering that it wasn't over. They could adopt a child, foster a child. He clenched his fists. Bastards like these, breeding, breeding...

'Please, Mister! Please!'

'What?' he said, harshly, but restraining his urge to swear at her. 'What?'

'Come an see, Mister.' And when he still didn't move, 'Please. Oh, please.'

She led him through the grass. The ground sloped here, down towards a stream that trickled from a concrete pipe into a steep concrete-sided channel leading down towards the river. Above them, the back gardens of Balmoral, a bank strewn with rubbish, pocked with little excavated caves. Tangles of bedsteads and shopping trolleys. There'd be rats here, nest after nest of them. The air was loud with flies. She kept turning to him, beckoning him as they descended. The heat and stench intensified. What could she want him for?

They came to the final slope, six feet of concrete that

dropped steeply to the stream. She stood at the brink, precarious, pointed down.

'There! Look, Mister. Down there!'

It was at the stream's edge, half in and half out of the water. A small sack tied with string. There was movement in it. Thin whining noises were coming from it.

He turned back to her, stared.

'Get them, Mister. Get them out.'

The dog stood stupidly, tongue hanging slack, dripping.

She reached out, took his hand, tugged at him.

'Mister...Mister...'

He could hardly breathe down here. The heat, the awful air.

'You can do it, Mister.' Encouraging him, persuading him. 'It'll be all right, Mister.'

'You bastards,' he whispered. 'Breeding, breeding...'

His head reeled. He recalled the consultant's office, how he had leaned down, pressed his eye to the microscope, stared down into the light... The sperms spun frantically, getting nowhere. They lay malformed, headless, tailless. They lay scattered, simply dead. He felt Alison's hand on his shoulder, heard her voice as she drew him back. Oh, love, she whispered. It'll be all right. There'll be something we can do. There must be something we can do...

'Please, Mister. Please!'

The consultant watched him. An infection, he said. An accident, maybe. At some time, something had gone wrong. Something that may have seemed trivial, hardly noticeable. Was there anything? Did he remember anything...?

'Mister!'

He raised his hands, a gesture of abandonment. He let the mail fall into the grass. He dropped to hands and knees at the edge, began slowly to swing himself over. As he let himself down, awkwardly braking his fall with feet, belly, knees, she urged him, soothed him.

'Go on,' she told him, and he let himself fall, ended on all fours in the stream…

The water was icy cold and clear, sparkling as it trickled from the mouth of the pipe. All around the mouth were ferns and creeping plants, trails of star-shaped blooms. Bright mosses were rooted on the channel. A brilliantly blue damselfly hovered there, above the tiny waterfall. The air was cooler, reflections of water danced in the shade at the side of the channel, on his bare arms. He looked up, saw the dog's head and the girl's head, the fervent eyes poised over him.

He turned, reached out towards the sack, but hesitated. The whining in there, the movement. With fingertips he gripped the string that fastened the sack, quickly tugged it clear of the water, and he crouched, staring.

'Let them out,' she told him. 'Mister! Let them out.'

He slid his hands under the sack and lifted it. He felt the weight of the animals inside. He felt their desperate limbs, frantic hearts. He felt tiny teeth and claws seeking an exit as he fumbled with the string, but he too was in a panic. He too was frantic, useless.

'Oh, Mister! Oh, Mister!'

He lifted the sack higher, held it up in both hands towards the girl and she reached out to take it from him, lifted the sack over the edge, turned from him...

He crouched again in the stream. He cupped his hands, lifted water to his head and face. He saw the damselfly, still hovering. Beyond it, beyond the ferns and mosses at the mouth, lay the blackness in the pipe beneath Balmoral. He trembled. He remembered nothing. He foresaw nothing. He imagined the world above him razed, bulldozed, bleached, the sun glaring on the last few mutants, the final twitches of life. He imagined heat, brightness, immobility, going on forever. The thought of such damage, the thought of such a hell inside himself...

'Oh, Mister! Mister! Mister!'

The voice was singing, echoing down into the channel.

'Come see, Mister!'

She was leaning down to him, offering her hand to him, and as he scrambled up the slope, shoved himself onto the grass, she tugged him, helping to drag him over.

The sack was open. The puppies were tiny, beige, almost yellow in the sunlight. They sprawled exhausted in the grass. The dog stood over them, nudging them, licking them. John knelt speechless, found himself wondering at the beauty of the pups, the ugliness of the dog, found himself gazing into the girl's face, seeing it so transfigured by delight.

'Aren't they so pretty?' she said. 'Aren't they so lovely?'

She took his hand, rested it on each of the puppies in turn.

'We saved them,' she said. 'Didn't we, Mister? Didn't we? You an me an Sabre! We saved them.'

'Yes,' he said. 'We saved them.'

He watched her with them, saw how delicate she was

with them. He reached out to her, touched her shoulders, cheeks, hair.

'Yes,' he whispered. 'You an me an Sabre. We saved them.'

She began lifting the puppies, trying to lay them in the crook of her arm, but she was too small, there wasn't room for them.

He slung the mail across his back, crooked his own arm, lay the puppies down on it, hushed them, soothed them.

'What will you do with them?' he asked.

'Just take them home. Look after them...'

She led the way, retracing the narrow path they'd worn through the long grass, and she kept turning to him, smiling. The dog followed, close behind. They heard the noise of children and their dogs coming from the gardens, the far-off noises of the sites. Above the river the cranes had begun to move across the sky.

They came back to the trenches and the cars, and as they approached the entrance he found the girl at his side, with her hand resting in his.

She led him in, and as they walked over the red writing he saw faces at the windows, watching. Children paused in the middle of their games. The dogs were out, roaming from garden to garden.

Somewhere a man was calling.

'Anna!' he called. 'Anna! Anna! Anna!' The voice echoed through the cul-de-sacs, across the greens, over the roofs.

The girl laughed.

'That's me,' she said.

'That's Dad,' she said.

He thought of the mail. He should deliver it now that he'd returned, but her hand, tugging him forward, was insistent.

'It's just down here,' she said. 'Just through here, Mister.'

One of the fully boarded places. On every board the red word NO. Still the man was calling, but from another house, another street. 'Anna! Anna! Anna!' She led him to the back of the house. The garden there looked out across bare flattened earth towards the wharves. The fence was reinforced with thick stakes hammered down into the grass. Tangles of barbed wire were nailed there. Rows of vegetables were growing, fruit bushes with tiny berries becoming visible amongst the green.

'Anna! Anna! Anna!'

The voice was troubled now.

'They think I'm gone,' she said.

'I'm here!' she yelled. 'Here I am!'

The back door was ajar. John laid the puppies in the grass, pushed the door further open. Breakfast things on a plastic table, the dog's bowl beneath. Behind the boards the windows were unbroken. He went in, shoved open another door, let light into the pitch-black living room. A few chairs arranged in a ring, at the centre a handful of eviction notices. Pasted on the window, newspaper reports of Balmoral's fight. On a sofa: a hatchet, a screwdriver, some carving knives.

Again she was calling.

'I'm here! Here I am!'

Her father's voice was closer.

He pulled the door shut, turned towards the garden. Sabre was in the doorway, teeth bared, growling.

'Sabre!' he said. 'Let me out, Sabre!'

'Anna!' he said.

There were footsteps at the side of the house. The dog became excited, began barking, howling, began coming in.

'Anna!' he said. 'Anna!'

He saw the man arrive outside. He saw him lean down and lift Anna into his arms.

'Anna!' he said. 'Anna, Anna! Where've you been, my love?'

She started giggling, dancing in his arms.

'For the puppies,' she said. 'Me an the postman an the dog!'

And she pointed in.

'Look! Look who I've brought home!'

And as he turned, John looked out in wonder from the darkness into the father's joyful eyes, while Anna just laughed and laughed, saying,

'Sabre! Stop it, you silly dog...'

NESTING

FOR YEARS HE'D PESTERED HER: TELL ME WHAT IT WAS LIKE WHEN I was in you. Tell me what it was like before I was here.

For years she'd told him. But as he grew older, he began never to ask. And she began only on bright mornings ever to tell.

It was spring. The streetlights were on. Blackbirds had stopped singing in the hedges.

'Stay inside,' she said. 'Just one night.'

He perched on the edge of his chair, with his jacket on his knee.

'Stephen!'

It was her pleading voice, the one he hated.

'Just goin f'ra while,' he muttered. 'Not long.'

'You'd protect me, Stephen. Soon as he went you said you would. Now I'll be the man, you said. The man.'

'An I will. Tellin y'I will.'

'Tellin's nothin. Stay inside.'

He crouched and fiddled with his shoelaces, fastening them viciously tight.

'They come through the windows, Stephen, even when you're in. Doesn't matter if you're in. They wait in the gardens for the men to leave. They come in quiet wi'their knives and snooker cues, wi'stockins on their faces. Woman keep still, they tell you. Not a move or you'll get what's comin. Where is it? they ask. Stephen, what'll I tell them when there's nowt?

'So what's to come for if there's nowt?'

'That's it. What they left with? Me. Nowt but me. Stephen, stay inside.'

'There's nobody, woman. Who'd wait to get in here?'

He followed the street's long curve, turned into the narrow alley that led him out through the fringes onto the waste. Out there the ground dropped, a sudden quickening of the miles-long slope towards the sea. Once there'd been a few streets here, almost a village. There were a few stone remnants blanketed by bramble and ivy, thin strips of garden still marked by rampant hedges. Spreading out from it was a circle of paltry spoil-heaps, and deep gashes in the earth that had become the estate's dumps. Years ago, with the other kids, he'd spend whole days roaming the hillside, searching the hedges for nests. The ruined streets had been their ghost town, where they'd play until the long scary shadows came and sent them running, filled with laughter and fright, back towards the brand new houses.

Now the other kids went other ways. They took buses into the city that was already burning the sky beyond the crest. They gathered in the estate's community centres and clubs. And, it was true, there were those who did prowl the curving streets, poised to take their chances.

He shuddered and went down, taking a narrow cindered track, ancient waggon way edged with its dense hawthorn hedges. He knew it all, even in the dark. After a quarter mile or so, he turned right, ducking through towards a cottage less dilapidated than most. It smelt of shit in there, and massive thistles grew out through the floor. But there were walls almost as tall as he was, with strips of bleached paper still attached behind the creepers. A single window frame remained, a square filled with the slope, the silhouettes of factories at the top, the burning sky. He lowered himself onto the collection of cushions and rags he'd months ago dragged from the dumps. He emptied his pockets: an aerosol, a plastic bag. He sprayed the aerosol until there was a pool in the corner of the bag. He wrapped the bag around his face and breathed deeply. He went on breathing, tightening the bag's opening against his cheeks, pushing his lips closer and closer, waiting for the darkness to deepen, for the thundering of blood to begin.

The day he left, she had Stephen singing. They sat together on the sofa, looking out into the street. Her voice started it:
'Clap hands for Daddy coming
Down the waggon way
His pockets full of money
And his hands all clay...'
She kept leaving him, scanning from the window, returning to him. She smiled. 'Come on, Stephen. What's wrong? Too big to sing now?' She took his hands, clapped them between her own.
'Clap hands for Daddy coming
Down the waggon way...'

They went on waiting as far as dusk and beyond. He lay against her breast and felt her trembling. 'Sing,' she whispered. 'Sing.'

He sang. He was twelve years old then. He'd been born here, when the estate was a riddle of foundation trenches, half-made roads, half-formed walls. His infancy had been accompanied by the clink of trowels, the suck and smack of pile drivers, the bulleting of pneumatic drills. On expeditions out, strapped into the Silver Cross that lurched on rubble and underfill, he stared out from beneath the dark hood to watch his mother cursing, grinning through her sweat, singing at him, calling to the foremen, 'Will it ever all be done?' She taught him the ring of streets, the alleyways out onto the slope, the wilderness outside, the distant sea. She showed him the factories being massively assembled around the crest. 'That's where Daddy'll go,' she told him. 'When it's all done, he'll be in there, workin the machines.' As he grew older, between the men going up in the morning and their coming back at night, he learned the dusty silence of the streets, the afternoons disturbed only by children playing, mothers calling, the endless droning from the crest. 'And's how it ought to be,' his father would say. 'Whole places made for them like us. Homes put here, work put here. So's it's all clean and new and settled f'ra change, and you feel you're worth somethin wi' a life worth lookin forward to. Right, lass? Bloody aye.'

Sundays he'd take Stephen out, leaving the Silver Cross to gleam uselessly in the kitchen. 'Mother's stuff,' he'd say. 'The lad's got legs. May's well learn from the start which way they'll be leadin him.' So the boy was half-led, half-dragged, with his arm held vertical by the man's fist, towards the new workplaces that even on Sundays were filled with the subdued beating of engines. Out here his father cursed freely, inviting the boy into a man's fellowship of work and sweat. 'Tired, kid? I bloody bet y'are. T's how it is. T's how it's always been for them like us.' He turned the boy's face towards each factory in turn. 'But we're winnin, kid. We made our claim, an look!'

After the singing, long silence and the dark. Her body trembling, sudden outbursts of her breath. She clenched him tight, tighter, till he slithered from her grip with,

'Mam! I cannot breathe.'

'Where's that man?' she whispered. 'Stephen, go and look.'

At the door he followed with his eyes the curve of streetlights, shadowed gardens, curtained panes.

She shouted at him, 'Well? Well?' She came up behind him, shoved his arms into a coat.

'Thinks we're nothin. Thinks he can do it, like he said he would. Can't, can he? Can't get away with it. We'll find the bugger, Stephen, bloody right we will. Out you go. Come on, bloody out!'

Out through an alleyway onto the dead straight road leading to the crest, cutting across a waste of weedy underfill towards the darkened factories. Nothing but a thin whining from them now, padlocked gates, massive loading doors sealed shut. At his place, beneath its shattered neon name, the one light came from a shed at arm's length inside the fence. She shoved her arm through, hammered at it. From inside a man's voice yelled at her to clear off home. She went on hammering, until its tiny window was opened and he yelled,

'Is that still you soddin kids?'

'It's me,' she told him. 'Me. Look. Just me, an the lad here.'

He angled his head through the open frame.

'What's wrong, woman? What you after?'

'Me man,' she said. 'I'm lookin for me man.'

'Oh, aye?'

'I want to know who's workin,' she said. 'If he's workin.'

'Workin? No bugger, only me. They finished ages past.'

'But if there's another shift... If they needed one to get it done...'

'Look around, woman. Listen.'

She pressed her face hard against the fence.

'Then where is he? Where's my man?'

The watchman stared at her. He sighed and spat.

'Go home, woman. There's more to worry him than bloody silly women an their kids.' The window slammed. They headed back to the estate. On the wasteland in between she picked up half-bricks, stones, and flung them out into the dark. Afterwards, they searched the pubs, didn't find him there.

Feathers and cotton clung to his skin. He drew his knees to his chest, squirmed into the rags. He was so cold. He would have to move.

He'd dreamed of going home one night to find her dying, the house ransacked, the bloodied snooker cue beside her head. But tonight was like most nights: opening the door to a room filled with the fierce heat of a gas fire, to her drunken sleep; leaving her there, going to stare from his window at the ring of lights surrounded by the dark; slipping towards unconsciousness again, towards the memory of his father, the last night he'd come in...

'Stevie! Stevie!' An urgent whisper, the man leaning over him, the door open to the landing's glare.

'Stevie! What's the matter wi'ye?'

Blinking, heart thundering, gasping for air.

'Stevie! It's me, lad. What's up wi'ye?'

'Nothin.' A garbled cry.

'So what ye laughin for?'

'Laughin? Dream, dad... Must've been a dream.'

'Bugger dreams, lad. Sleep, lad. Eh?'

'Yes, dad.'

'No dreams now, eh?'

'No, Dad...'

The man turning to leave, but hesitating, pushing the door to, returning through the darkness to the bed. Crouching low, his lips hard by the boy's ear, his whisper cracking with its angry edge,

'This is how they get you, this is how they lie to you. Look at this, they tell you. Isn't it grand, isn't it what you've always wanted? Get you when you're daft, half-asleep, when they tell you, Good lad, always knew you were a good'n. Gan on, they say, Smile. Look what we've got you. Gan on, lad, take it...

Bastards! Get you when you're dreamin, son, get you when you're soft. And not long till they've got what they wanted and they're telling you, No! Leave off! Get back to where you were! Back in your box, bird brain. Yours? Wors. Wors all the time. Not for the likes o'you. Piss off back to sleep. Leave it!... You know what I'm sayin, son?'

Stephen lay as if he couldn't move, breathing low, his heart racing.

'Get out, Stevie. That's me meanin. That's the thing to do. Get out quick's you can. Soon as there's a space, start runnin. They'll try to stop you. Nice lad, they'll say. Always been a good'n. Come here, look at this, they'll say. Don't believe them, Stevie. Tell them, Stevie: Piss off wi'your lies! Aye? Stevie!'

Huge hands gripped Stephen's head, twisted it towards the dark face.

'Stevie! Tell me aye. Bloody aye!'

'Yes...yes...aye...,' the words coming suddenly, on each panted breath.

'Good lad, Stevie. That's the way. When they come to you, just tell them no.'

The hands relaxed. The face dipped towards him, kissed him.

'Good lad. You'll be all right. Just gan to sleep. That's right, son. That's right... love.'

Nothing more, except, as the man moved towards the door, the final words, 'An don't marry. Don't fall for that lot, either,' and later, the ferocious voices of both of them, man and woman, stretching deep into the night.

'... an he'd lean over, from where you're sittin now, an he'd lay his whole hand flat across me belly – like this, look. Just to feel you. Just to feel the kickin of you. An he'd swear – you know, the way he did. Bugger, he'd say. Feel it growin, gettin strong. He'd keep on askin, How big's it, how big's it now? An when he'd had a drink he'd come an lay his head on me and he'd whisper at you and whistle for you. He'd be that daft – like a kid that cannot wait. Howay, little'n, he'd say. Howay out an play wi'us. You never knew him, Stephen – not when he was young and full of everythin. I've got it all, he used to say, an, Me an you, love, we've got it all...'

Mornings were calm, comparatively lucid. When the sun shone and the blackbirds sang, she'd lift a table into the small back garden and they'd breakfast there, facing each other, their knees almost touching. Her words each time searched the same themes: the past, his father, the building of the estate and the factories. But her stories had never become tedious to him. Though he never met her eyes, and hardly spoke except to mutter yes or no when asked if he, too, remembered, he was alert to every word, bringing as it did some answer to his prompting of years ago: Tell me what it was like...'

'...it was spring when you were growin fastest. Felt some days like you were takin all the strength from me, an all I could do was lie an let him fuss round me. Days when I was stronger he'd take me out onto the waggon ways an we'd walk an walk, right down past the tips an dumps. What a change there'd be down there, where you could lose yourself in the lanes an hedges. It was the silence of it all, when up here there was all day long the trucks an drills an engines. An wi' the plans they had, seemed like it would go on always, like there'd be no stop to it, like the estates would just keep spreadin and spreadin... But it weren't to be... Comin back, I'd have to hold him tight, let him take me weight. Take it easy, love, he'd say. An he'd let me stop an get me breath while he climbed right into the hedges lookin for nests an shouting back about the eggs an little'ns he'd found. An many's the time I came back here wi'a warm hedgesparrow's egg in me hand or a chaffinch's in me pocket...'

Her voice faded. Soon, he knew, it would deepen, she'd begin to search her other theme, of how it all went wrong. She held him as he tried to move away.

'We watched you growin straight an strong and he'd laugh an say, The jammy sod – born now, best of all times to be born...'

From inside, through the kitchen window, he watched her head fall forward. He shivered. She'd start on the bad times, the changes. 'It broke his heart, Stevie. It changed him. It started him sayin we shouldn't've started any of it, we shouldn't've met, we shouldn't've come here. He started watchin you an sayin we shouldn't've had you, it might all have been easier if we hadn't've had you...'

'Stevie!' She had turned to him, and he saw that the morning's light hadn't entirely drained from her eyes. 'An your eggs! You remember them? Boxes an boxes o'them underneath your bed. All that bright blue an the white an the dark patches. An how he loved you even then? How he'd sit wi'you an hold them wi'you and keep tellin you what this one was an this one was...'

'Aye,' said Stephen, moving from the window, heading out. He did remember – the man's gentle touch as he fingered the hollow shells and the pinholes; how he turned his face from the boy as he muttered that this was maybe the best way,

'Spat out like so much snot – never to be born at all.'

Some days he still went out like this, as if he were still dragged by his father's fist. He ascended the hill, passed the silent factories, squatted among the heather and rocks at the crest. He kept jamming a tin of lighter fluid to his nostril, squeezing. Icy-cold, breath-stopping, but with an almost immediate thrill that sent his mind reeling. The estate hunched in on itself behind back gardens and fences. The broken ground at its fringes contained trenches and heaps of underfill, remnants of long-abandoned building projects, weeds that each spring were higher and more dense. He saw his father's arms widening as he described what was to come, filling the space with houses and workplaces going on for ever. He saw his father in a rage, coming out from the factories, running to the crest, setting off on the miles-long ribbon of road towards the city, yelling, 'No. Bloody no!' One day he'd follow him... Thin mucous was draining from him. He sniffed, spat. He'd said no, months ago. They'd come to him, wanting him for their schemes and projects, with, 'He's a good lad, is Stephen. We'll train him. We'll give him what he needs.' He watched them, silent. Lies, he thought. They were tender, telling him he'd change things for his mother and himself. She'd been with him, had turned to him, her eyes widening with anticipation. 'No!' he'd yelled at her. 'Bloody no!'... He spat again. He stood up, began his descent. All across the hillside the work of those who'd said yes was starting: neat signposts at the junctions of the waggon ways, trimmed and newly laid hedges, turfed spoil heaps. They'd get to his cottage, raze it. They'd clear the estate's fringes. There'd be playgrounds and picnic spots. On the crest there'd be parking places and benches. Children on tiptoe would peer through telescopes as far as the sea. You could be part of all this, they'd told him. You'll help the whole place to be re-born. People will want this place, will want to come. 'Stephen,' she'd whispered – her whining voice. 'No!' he'd yelled. 'Bloody no!'

He veered past the estate onto his familiar cindered track. He started when the hedge started. He ducked into the dark, climbed, balanced in the forks of the boughs, peered towards the tips, heard all around him the mothers, filled with fright, clattering towards the sky. Nests: so many of them, deep inside the foliage, held and protected by spreading twigs and branches. He stretched, reached up, dipped his fingers into the first: a blackbird's, with its smooth and cupped inside. Three eggs. He lifted them one by one, placed them gently into his free hand's open palm. For a moment he regarded them, their blueness, their dark speckles. For a moment he heard the familiar voice from below: In your mouth, lad. Rest it on your tongue where it's warm and safe. He closed his fist tight. He sniffed, wiped his hand on his clothes, began again. The nests he couldn't reach he brought down, kicking and wrenching the branches that supported them until they splintered and snapped. He moved slowly, stepping from tree to tree, balancing, staring, reaching. All afternoon he worked. Occasionally he rested, squatting in a wide fork and holding the lighter fluid to his nose. Once, in a strong tree, he climbed so high that his head emerged from the foliage and he stared back, saw how short a space, compared with the miles of hedgerow that crossed the slope, he'd dealt with. But he didn't relent, went back into the dark, went back to leaving the ground and the branches scattered with smashed eggs, with young birds cheeping uselessly for their parents, went back to telling himself, 'Better like this. Aye, better like this...'

At dusk, he dropped to the track. He marked the place with a pile of stones. He shuffled through to his cottage, curled up in there. His clothes were ripped, his skin torn. Tiny fragments of shell had attached themselves to every part of him. He took out the lighter fluid once more. Nothing left except a vapour. It brought no thrill. He didn't reel. But he slept, and entered a darkness deeper than any there'd ever been out here in the waste; darkness with the thudding of blood in it and with a voice from outside coming closer, asking, 'How big's it? How big's it now?' and going on to call him, 'Little'n! Little'n! Howay out an play wi'us...'

They hadn't come. There was no bloodied snooker cue. She was sleeping on the sofa, facing the gas fire. He stood staring, this boy coated with shell and feathers and with hollow eyes. He didn't want to leave, didn't want the whisper or the landing's glare. She didn't move. He turned off the light, turned off the fire, lay down with her. Without waking, she moved to accommodate him, allowed him to curl up close against her belly. They stayed all night. He kept waking. He kept promising her,

'I'll protect you, Mam. I'll stay inside...'

1962

THESE THINGS HAPPENED SO LONG AGO. FOR ANYTHING AT ALL TO happen then, there needed to be the pretty ones, and there needed to be the beasts. There were Daniel and Askew, my friends; my mother, who was taken from us at the start; the tramp, who came soon afterwards to live in our dunes. And there was me, and there was my father, living somewhere in the spaces in between.

*

It started soon after she was taken. It was a Sunday. I was asleep, dreaming her, and my father's voice, from outside the house, woke me. I lay listening, trying to understand, trying to distinguish the other voice, the unfamiliar. By the time I was at the window, this other, with black greatcoat hanging leaden to his heels and the beret jammed to his skull, was leaving. He tucked a parcel into his khaki kitbag, stepped down onto the beach, didn't look back.

Downstairs, at the table, my father muttered at me, cursed me.

'Twice I called you. Twice you answered: I'm coming... Yes, I'm coming.'

I remembered none of it. I poured honey from a spoon

onto my bread, watched the trembling patterns it made beneath my dead still hand.

'Look at the time. You might as well have stayed up there. It's nothing to you, is it? Or if it is, then it's nothing but a dream.'

I tried to turn away, tried to focus on the sea's horizon, but this was before he had learned that his terror could be silent, and he took my head in his hand, twisted me to him.

'Well?' he asked me. 'Well?'

I said nothing, waiting for him to release me, and it was only when his hands fell to the table that I whispered, 'Who was it, at the door this morning?' and he whispered in bitter reply, 'Jesus Christ, Tom! Is that all you can come up with? Jesus bloody Christ!'

Before we left for the hospital, I slipped out to the gate. I crossed the track, stood above the beach, gazed north towards the lighthouse, south towards the docks. No one but the coal collectors and their ponies, the usual children digging in the sand, a dog, spurred on by its master, leaping at the waves.

On the bus, he sat with his arm round me. He smoked cigarette after cigarette and I felt his bursts of coughing, suddenly controlled. The bus was filled with a transistor's tinny noise, playing all the way to Newcastle, and each time The Beatles sang I felt the leaping of my heart, the desire to pull away from him, laughing. He was silent until we entered the city and he pointed down across the traffic. 'Look,' he said. 'You remember that?'

'The Memorial,' I said, and I blushed, recalling again the embarrassment he'd brought me the previous November, the way he'd stood stock-still through the praying and the hymns, the way his voice had rung out above all others into the surrounding silent streets. She'd been with us then, had stood behind me with her hands gentle on my shoulders and her singing calm and sweet. Afterwards, when he went to drink for an hour with his friends, she took me walking by the river. 'Poor Tom,' she said. 'One day you'll understand. It was so awful, worse than anything there'll ever be again.' And then she laughed, and kissed me, and said that we were free of all that, and on the bridges we loosened our coats, gripped our hats, raced each other, yelling, 'Beat you to the other side!'

*

In the ward, we stood waiting for her to wake. He kept smoothing my hair with his licked palm. He whispered, 'Don't let her see that we've been quarrelling so much.' In the end, I leaned down to her, moved my fingers gently on her brow. 'Oh, Tom!' she exclaimed, before her eyes were even open. 'But look,' she said. 'You've grown so tall.' She made me stand beyond the bed's foot while he held her forward. 'Every time a little taller.' And she smiled, a fading smile as he lowered her to the pillows again. 'And look at me,' she said. 'Now I'm the little one. So tiny.' I sat at her feet. She kept drifting to sleep, waking, scolding herself. 'I can't seem to stay,' she whispered, her voice now more breath than articulation. 'What will become of me?' It was as if she was disappearing before our eyes. I wanted to reach beneath the covers, to touch her, to reassure myself that the ever-narrowing ridge beneath the covers was truly her. I'd already dreamed of finding nothing there, and I'd also dreamed of coming here at night, sitting on the starched sheets by her, telling her, 'It's nothing. You're only becoming little again. You'll shrink to a baby's size and you'll start all over again. It's what happens these days. I'll take care of you.' And I laughed and said, 'Just look at the size of me!' It seemed so easy. Next time I dreamed she was a baby, lying asleep, her nightgown a vast christening robe arranged across the bed. I carried her away from the hospital and the city, brought her to our beach. I lowered her into the waves, shouted her baptism to the coal gatherers, and she came out wailing, filled with life.

As we were leaving, the Sister spoke to my father in her room. 'The treatment,' she whispered. 'I know. It's almost another disease itself. But it's all we have to fight with.' He stood with his head turned down, his fists loosely clenched at his sides. 'Is there nothing we can do?' he asked her. 'Is there nowhere else we can take her?'

She let her hand rest on his shoulder.

'You must let her see that you are calm.'

*

'These'll be no good, you know,' said Daniel, once Askew and I had finally wrestled each other breathlessly to the sand. We'd been racing, leaping the huge concrete cubes that lined the foreshore. 'No bloody good at all,' he said. The cubes lined this whole beach, lined all the beaches to the north.

They were sinking, some of them were already half-buried in the sand. The only gap was at the centre of the bay, where the coal gatherers had dragged one of the cubes aside in order to make an entrance and exit for their ponies.

He stood with his hands in the pockets of his white shorts, his hooped jersey slopping down across his hips. He looked down at us. 'There'll be no landing craft, no tanks. It'll be guided missiles next time. It'll just be an ordinary day – dead silent, and then...'

'Shut up, Daniel,' said Askew, standing up, shaking the sand from his clothes. 'You're talking shite. It'll not happen. Never.'

Daniel just shrugged at that, said, 'Ban the bomb, that's what I say. And bloody quick, too.'

Askew snorted, and led us off in the direction of the lighthouse. 'Get rid of him,' he muttered. 'I don't know what you see in him.' But I shook my head. 'It's because he's new here. You'll get used to him.'

It was mid-afternoon, high tide, and the beach was deserted. The water was hardly moving beneath a steel sky. We came to the little headland that marked the limit to our bay. Beyond it was the marsh and the little copse of pine trees, then the long stretch of higher, wilder dunes, where the pitmen's tiny, brightly painted holiday huts nestled in the hollows. Behind it all, stretching back inland, were the villages and their dark spoil heaps, their pitheads black etchings in the afternoon's grey haze.

Daniel and I perched on the rocks beneath the lighthouse. Askew stood further out, grinning, thrusting his hips forward, pissing far out into the sea. Daniel inspected the surface of the rocks. With his small fingers he traced the inscriptions carved into the dark stone. He murmured names and dates. They were all around us, the deep inscriptions of the dead. '1902,' he said. '1898. Tom – 1860! A hundred years, and still not washed away.' I nodded, and showed him my namesake, Thomas 1882, Thomas 1905, the second written in a smaller, plainer script, and wondered again if the Thomases could be the same. Then Askew came, buttoning his fly, with his story of the stone beneath the water line, with a dozen Askews on it, going two centuries into the past.

'Two centuries,' he said, and I saw the glare in his eye. 'Two hundred years of being here.'

Then he stopped, and stood staring back inland.

'Who's this bugger?' he whispered, and both Daniel and I stood to stare with him.

He was moving away from us, across the marsh. He was dressed as before – the greatcoat, the beret. The kit bag was lashed diagonally across his back. He moved awkwardly, attempting to keep clear of the more sodden places, but he kept sticking, and he had to keep pulling himself free.

'He came to our place, begging,' I said.

We moved off the rocks, onto the turf that topped the headland. The man was clear of the marsh, had begun weaving his way through the pine trees. Soon he was into the dunes, and lost in them.

'He asked for work,' said Daniel. 'They let him help to dig the drains.'

'Did they, by God?' whispered Askew, and again I saw

the fire in his eyes, but Daniel continued,

'He was there all afternoon, breaking through to the old ones. Then they fed him, and sent him off with some bread and some cold tea. He stank of seaweed. They said he was half crazy.' He turned to me. 'He was harmless, though wasn't he, Tom?'

I caught my breath.

'I hardly saw him. My dad gave him something, I think. Not much.' I watched Askew. 'What do you think?' I asked him.

He didn't answer, but just stared at me, then said suddenly,

'OK. Let's move.'

We left Daniel behind. He wouldn't come. Askew cursed him as we splashed through the marsh. 'You want to be careful, you know,' he told me. 'Swine like him'll change you.' In among the pines I realised how the light was fading, how late it was becoming. 'I'll have to be back before long,' I told him. On the dunes the sand kept collapsing beneath our feet, and in places we had to climb on all fours, grip the sharp-edged marram grass, and when we rested I saw that my hands were crisscrossed by long thin lacerations, lines of tiny bulbs of blood. There was no sign of the man's footprints in the sand. 'He could have gone anywhere,' I said, looking past the huts towards the north, to where the landscape and the beaches became ever more barren, ever more wild. 'What time will it be?' I asked him. He led me on. Each time we came upon a hut, he peered through its tiny windows, rattled its locks. 'There's children come here in summertime,' he said. 'Don't want some old get like him lying in wait for them.' But in the end he just stopped, and cursed, and stood on the highest of dunes with his hands on his hips, shouting, 'Come on out, tramp! Filthy bastard, come on out!' I turned away from him and led the way back, tumbling down onto the shore, trailing towards the pines. All the way, Askew was cursing, saying, 'We'll get the bastard. We'll drive him out.' The tide was ebbing, the wet beach shone brilliantly beneath black clouds that streamed in from the horizon. As we approached the pines we saw Daniel, the white bloom of his shirt upon the rocks. Askew held me back, pointed to him. 'Look at it,' he whispered. 'Little nancy boy, still waiting. Little girly, sitting on the rocks.' I ignored him, moved in silence through the marsh. On the other side, he grabbed me, and his voice was thrilled, trembling. 'Now,' he whispered. 'Let's get him now.' But I pulled free, and soaked to the knees and with my heart thundering, I started running. Behind me in the dusk I heard Askew growling, Daniel's yelps of pain. But it was so late. Already the house was locked and empty. I followed the lane towards the village. At the centre, the small square of shops arranged around the fountain, I began to weep. The bus was leaving, was already heading out through the narrow streets on the other side. From the brilliantly lit upstairs deck, a face I knew must be that of my father was peering back at me through tunnelled hands.

*

We were on the beach together, my mother and I, when first it showed itself. An icy February day with the whole sea churning. She kept pulling me to her, wrapping me round with the huge sleeves of her woollen coat, laughing at the absurdity of living in such a place. 'He said we'd go everywhere!' she shouted, raising her voice against the din of waves and wind. She ran to the water's edge, tiptoed rapidly backwards when the water rushed towards her feet. She raged at the sea's coldness, its blackness, but her face, as she flung handfuls of sodden sand and coal into the waves, was filled with delight. 'That man of ours!' she yelled. 'What a fraud! It was to be Canada this, Australia that! Oh, yes, that was the style! A whole world waiting! Free as birds! We'll sharp be out of this hole, eh?' And she took my hand and danced me back and forth along the shore with, 'Come on, Tom, my lovely Tom. Dance yourself away with me.' She rushed me to the shelter of the cubes, and, 'Look,' she whispered, taking from her purse a tiny square photograph of herself, holding it cupped in her palms. The print had lost all whiteness, but she smiled out, beautiful, from beneath the darkening of all the years between. In it she was sixteen, and beneath the curls her face appeared an image of my own, as if she were some unknown sister, or some alternative version of myself. 'This is the only me that's been, or's going anywhere,' she laughed. 'Silly man. He took it out with him to Egypt, carried it all the way back. Said he'd have done without tin hat or rifle before doing without that. Angel, he called me when he'd made it back. Guardian angel. And then he gave it back to me to keep it safe.' I reached into her hands to lift it, but the wind rushed in between us, caught the photograph, sent it spinning out onto the open beach, and, 'Oh, Tom!' she yelled, as I sprinted after it, 'Oh catch it, Tom!' I caught it a hundred yards away at the water's edge. It was face down, clinging to the wet sand, and when I lifted it, already the dampness had begun to seep in from its edges. She welcomed me back with applause and, 'How quick you are, my Tom!' but when she slipped the picture back into her purse, I saw in her eyes how truly scared she'd been. 'It's all right,' I told her. 'It'll dry. It'll be just like it was.' I took her hand and we stepped up onto the rough ground above the beach. The wind was clattering last year's weeds, was whipping at her coat. She kept stumbling. 'Damned weather,' she muttered. 'Damned place. Hold tight, Tom. Hold me tight.'

That afternoon I ministered to her. I carried warm drinks and blankets to her, heaped coal onto the fire, but I couldn't seem to warm her until I knelt and held her feet, tucked them beneath my pullover. We smiled at that and when my father came in, she was asleep at last.

'We went on the beach,' I told him. 'It was icy cold.'

'Aye,' he said, and with the back of his fingers he touched her brow. 'She's sickening for something.'

We sat silent, at opposite sides of the fire. At six-o-clock he switched on the television with its sound low. There'd been nuclear tests in Russia. In America, Kennedy shuffled the papers on his lectern, whispered quickly to one of his generals, then spoke of his resolution, of our growing strength. There were no limits, he told us, to the steps we'd take.

The voices woke her, and she stared at the two of us, her eyes filled with surprise.

'Fancy!' she whispered. 'After all that worrying, being scared of losing everything, to find myself with all of this. I think I'd like to go upstairs now, my loves.'

He went to her, lifted her, and we all smiled at her familiar lightness, her smallness. As he carried her out, she grinned back at me over his shoulder. She winked at me. 'Australia,' she said, and she giggled at the word. 'Australia!'

While they were gone, I retrieved the picture from her purse. A wide blister of damp had spread across her face. I laid it on the mantelpiece, stood staring at my own face in the mirror above, imagined curls falling to my shoulders, imagined brave and teasing eyes. Soon he came to my side.

'It's a chill,' he told me. 'Nothing more.'

He lifted the photograph. With his index finger he smoothed sea salt and speckles of coal dust from its surface. He laughed. 'She said you'd have swum to Germany to get it back. Look at her, son. She was really something, eh?'

Later that evening the wind fell. The sound of the sea was a regular slap and hiss of small waves. He went on watching TV. I told him that I'd go walking for a while and he nodded, asked if I didn't mind if he didn't come with me this time. Outside, a huge moon had lifted over the horizon. Far out, the tiny lights of trawlers headed north. I kept to the lane, walking towards the village. At its edge I turned inland, to Daniel's place where I climbed the garden wall and crouched in the shadows, staring in. They'd installed a window that fell almost to ground level. Inside, the walls had been stripped back to the bare stone. Furniture and wooden crates were stacked against the walls. Daniel was perched among these, reading a magazine. His parents lounged on the single sofa, laughing, feet stretched out towards the electric fire. There was music, the complicated, incomprehensible sounds of jazz, and I watched Daniel nodding his head to it, swaying his shoulders. When it ended, his father stood up. He was dressed in jeans, a huge green pullover that covered his hips. He leaned over the record player, holding his hair back with his hands, and positioned a stack of singles above the turntable. Now I knew the wailed introduction, the insistent voices:

If there's anything that you want,

If there's anything I can do...

Inside, Daniel was dancing. I got to my feet and climbed back into the lane. The moon was higher now, above the centre of the sea, filling the surface with its light. I began to run, over the rough ground, over the concrete defences, onto the sand. I pulled off my shoes and waded through the water and its ever-present bits of swirling black. I tugged at my hair, twisted it around my fingertips. 'It'll be just like it was,' I insisted. 'It will be. Just like it was.'

*

The man had been again. This time I'd seen him coming. I was at my window, watching for Askew. I scanned the beach and saw him at the rocks. He came slowly, toeing the weed and jetsam. Occasionally he stooped to the sand, inspected something, lifted it, until he turned away from the water and headed for us. I saw him for the first time plainly, saw the black eyes in the white exhausted face, the lips a bloody gash between white whiskers, the hair hanging wild below the tight beret. At the gate, he caught me staring, and he hesitated. I edged backwards into the room, seeing the sudden lifting of his chin, his nod, his acknowledgement. Dead still, I listened to the muffled negotiations from below, returned in the silence afterwards to the window. From the lane outside, while he stuffed his paper parcel into his coat, he looked again, gave his acknowledgement again. My father came to join me, put his hand on my shoulder and we watched him moving on.

'Poor soul,' he said. 'Gave all he had and look what he's been brought to.' He held me tighter. 'What's wrong?' he asked.

'Nothing. It's what he could get up to, though. What he could do. There's children...'

He was laughing, indulgent, tender.

'What he could do? He hardly knows his own name, never mind how to harm. He was in Singapore, Tom. Any harm was whipped out of him years ago.'

He took me downstairs, where he had soup waiting.

'It's not the likes of him that's dangerous,' he said. 'It's the others, the ones that came through and that've still got it in them. The ones that's waiting for the chance to start it all again. You can hear them anywhere, any day. Listen.'

And he switched on the news, and sure enough they started, the voices talking of war, threatening war.

'This isn't enough for them,' he whispered. 'This peace, this quiet. Listen to them – animals, howling for blood.'

Afterwards, we swept and dusted the living room together. I polished the window, staring through, watching for Askew. The air was filled with shimmering pinpricks of dust.

'We'll keep it lovely for her!' he exclaimed. 'I'll carry her in and she'll say, Oh, haven't you been so good!'

I saw Askew coming through the lane. He had a long stick, he kept beating the weeds, sending the seeds high around him.

'She will come?' I whispered.

'Oh aye, Tom. One way or another, they'll send her home.' And he came and hugged me so tight I was almost in pain. 'And isn't that a day to look forward to?'

Askew didn't even ask me. He just told me we were going back into the dunes.

'Christ!' he said, striding on the firm sand by the water, 'Have you seen him, close to? Have you smelt him? I kept my distance, but he's a fucking nightmare, Tom. And the stink of him! Like something rotten. Like somebody already dead.' And in the marsh he stopped, stared down at the saturated ground, cursed again. 'And when he was past,' he said, 'When he was past I was shaking. Fucking shaking. Like this, look. Just like this.'

On the dunes, I saw that he was burning with desire. With his face inflamed, and his feet thumping on the turf and sand, he moved so quickly I struggled in his wake. We went further this time, to where there were fewer pathways and fewer, meaner huts. 'This is where he'll be,' he told me. 'Keep your eyes peeled, Tom. This is where he'll be.' We moved slowly. We prowled. I was trembling. I kept looking back, in terror of

finding him already with us. But it was I who found his place,
on a steep, landward slope of the dunes. I saw the driftwood,
stacked high beside a charred hole in the earth, then the hut,
a clumsy arrangement of floorboards and railway sleepers
half-buried in the sand. Askew embraced me. 'You're bloody
beautiful!' he said, and he pulled me, led me down. The
windows were shuttered. Inside, in the building's single room,
by the light of the open door, we saw blankets drawn neatly
over a timber bed. A spindly table, bleached almost white,
bore a few crusts, a tin mug with tea dregs in it. There was a
chipped enamel bowl by the door, some tattered magazines.
Nothing more. I stood in the doorway while Askew went to
the bed, lifted its covers back. 'Oh, Christ,' he whispered. 'The
stench of it.' I moved further into the dark, smelled nothing
but seaweed and damp sand, a lingering scent of creosote.
'What is it?' I asked. He flung the covers right back, making
gagging noises in his throat. 'Can you not smell it, Tom?' he
asked me. 'Christ, Tom, can you not smell?'

We went back out into the air. Askew spat, cleared his
throat, spat again. I peered south, watching for him, expecting
him. 'He'll be coming,' I said. Askew was stamping the earth,
beating his foot regularly into the sand. 'Yes,' he told me.
'Yes. I know.' Suddenly he reached forward and turned my
face towards his. 'We've got to do something,' he said. 'We
can't let him just go on like this.' 'Like what?' I answered, but
he ignored me and knelt in the sand outside the doorway.
He smoothed the sand with his palm, began writing in it. NO
TRAMPS ALLOWED HERE. NO ANIMALS. 'That's what he
is, Tom,' he said as I pulled him away. 'A bloody beast.'

1962

On the way back we kept to the beach. It seemed to take an age. The tide was coming in, massive waves were crashing on the rocks. Now it was I who walked quickly, wanting to be away from here and into the safety of our own bay. We were almost at the pines when we saw him coming through, and I gasped, 'Askew!' But Askew simply came to a halt, and stood his ground as the man approached then passed within ten yards of us. For a second he turned to us, tilting his head back in order to peer through his tangled hair, and then continued, climbing up into the dunes, not looking back. 'Oh, Christ,' whispered Askew, with his voice trembling, and all the way to my door he was filled with excitement, cursing, drumming his fists on his hips, telling me, 'We'll get him now, Tom. We'll get the bugger now.'

At the gate he held me. He gazed deep into my eyes.

'Daniel!' he whispered. 'Daniel?' I said. 'The little girly boy. He'll get the bugger going. He'll bring him down.'

Inside the house, my father and I hurried our meal. 'Been far?' he asked me, and I shook my head.

'The beach,' I said, and he told me to hurry, to go and change. 'We saw the tramp again,' I said.

He was fiddling with the buttons of the TV.

'Go on,' he said. 'Please.'

'Have you smelt him?' I said.

'Smelt him? Smelt what? Do it, son. Please.'

I washed and changed quickly. I took a moment to stare into the dusk, right back to where the hut was. I shivered, imagined the man reading the sand. Downstairs, father switched off the television. 'Tom!' he yelled.

We ran side by side to the square, climbed into the empty
bus. As we set off, he shook his head.

'Cuba!' he said. 'Bloody Cuba!'

I stared at him.

'Cuba. It's where they're starting it.'

*

We spent all morning preparing for her. I soaped the window
frame and the door. I stretched full length beneath the bed,
seeking dust and dirt. He pulled off the covers, polished the
metal bedhead and bedfoot, fiercely brushed the mattress,
and together we lay starched white sheets across the bed,
wrapped plump pillows in starched white cases. I ran out,
brought in the year's last campions, white from the ground
above the beach, red from beneath the garden hedges. 'We'll
have to be so careful with her, Tom,' he said, 'So gentle,' and
he inspected his hands as if they might be clumsy with her, as
if they might harm her. He emptied her wardrobe, began re-
folding her things, and out of them fell her photograph to the
floor, and she lay there looking up at us through the blisters
and the cracks, ever smiling. He let me take it, watched as I
slipped it into my shirt pocket, whispered, 'That's right, Tom.
Keep her safe.'

I couldn't settle. Downstairs, I kept returning to the
window, watching the lane. 'It'll be ages yet,' he told me. 'Go
on out. Walk some of that energy away.' Out there, I prowled
a narrow patch of the beach, my senses all alert for her.
Daniel came, and he was filled with the coming war. 'Look,'

he said, kneeling in the sand, drawing with a dried-out piece of driftwood, 'This is where the bloody Yanks are, circling Cuba. These are the Russians, coming in. They won't turn back, Tom. Not now. Not after all they've said.' He took hold of my arm. 'There's nothing we can do. A few more days and it could all be over. Nothing left. Tom?'

I'd turned away from him to face the lane.

'She's coming home today,' I said, and he cursed and stepped closer to me, put his arms around me. I let him hold me and he whispered, 'She must be better, Tom. She must be well.' He waited with me for an hour or more, and he kept attending to me with words of reassurance, setting up games for us – tossing stones at debris, making pictures in the sand – but all the time he kept turning his eyes towards the sky, scanning the horizon. 'It's how it'll start,' he said. 'Suddenly. No warning.' Then he left me, whispering, 'Take care,' as Askew came along the shore.

'Aye,' said Askew, mocking him, 'He knows there's something up. You didn't tell him, Tom? Good lad, good mate.' I shuffled back towards the house. 'It'll do no harm, you know,' he said. 'We get Daniel there. The beast thinks he's beautiful. He can't control himself. He attacks. We're the witnesses, Tom. Whatever happens, we tell the tale. And they have to do something, have to get rid of him.'

I clenched my fists.

'But why should Daniel do it?' I said.

'Why? Because we'll fucking make him, mate.'

'Oh, Askew,' I groaned, at the same time seeing the ambulance behind him coming along the lane and I stood

David Almond

stock-still, hearing nothing more that Askew said, while they opened the doors and carried her in.

'She's home,' I whispered. 'Let me go.' And he turned round in surprise.

"That's great," he said. 'You'll be your old self again now.' She was already in the bed, and she composed a teasing smile for me as I walked in, but her face was pale as the white campions, her eyes as bruised as the red. Soon her features settled back into exhaustion, and we crouched on either side of her, linked arms across the tiny ridge of her body. 'It'll be so much better now,' she whispered. 'It'll be just like it was.'

'Yes,' I whispered, wanting to feed her, to nourish her, to bring her back to bloom, but within minutes she was sleeping, hardly breathing.

That night I kept staring from my bed towards the stars. I listened, but there were only the gentle waves, my father snoring. Then I heard her groans, and I dreamed again of being on starched sheets with her. She was suddenly huge, swollen with life. I delivered the child for her, and when I placed it in the space between us, I saw that it was she who was the child. I lifted her again, left the husk of her body on the bed. I ran into the night, splashed on the tideline, giggling and free, yelling Australia!, feeling her in my arms and her long curls dancing at my throat.

When I woke, the sun was streaming in at the window. The tide was far out, the sky was featureless, the whole world was still. I padded across the landing, peeped in at their door, saw her twisted at the bed's foot, sleeping, gasping for air. Downstairs I found my father in the kitchen. He leaned forward at the sink, gripping its edge. He didn't turn. 'Oh, my God, Tom,' he said, his voice deeper than it had ever been. 'Oh, Tom.' Then he growled and I looked out, saw the tramp coming in at our gate. 'Today?' I said. 'The beast? The bloody beast?' And I grabbed a kitchen knife, threw the door open, stepped out at him. 'No tramps!' I said, pointing the knife to his head. 'You understand? No tramps here!' He tilted his head back and turned his empty gaze into my eyes. 'No!' I said. 'Not here. No animals here.' And as he left I flung the knife uselessly towards the sea, heard it rattling the weeds beyond the lane.

I drew my father away from the sink. 'She will be fine,' I told him. 'It's up to us. We'll do it. We'll make her like she was.'

I went back up with him and we woke her. He lifted her from the awful bed and went to bathe her. Hardly able to breathe, I stripped off yesterday's sheets. I'd returned with fresh ones when he carried her back in. She was humming Beatles tunes, her eyes were shining, and she whispered, 'Won't it be lovely, my Tom, once we're free of all this?'

*

It was early afternoon. The coal gatherers had come down and they stood in the waves, sifting the sand. I sat watching the familiar rise and fall of the water. I gazed north towards the lighthouse, south towards the docks. I understood her now: this was a narrow, constraining place. The same landscape, same faces. When Daniel came I simply let him sit with me, let him talk of the immense sky. 'You won't see them,' he told me. 'But you can't stop yourself from watching for them. It'll mean the end of all of this.' Even when Askew came, and I found myself sitting between them, Daniel stayed. 'There's nothing to do now,' he had said. 'Nowhere to go.' I could feel Askew burning. In the moments he was silent, I took out her photograph, held it cupped in my palms. Then he started. 'I saw him,' he said. 'He was in beside the fountain. He had his hands full of fucking bread, a big bottle of tea. I shouted at him. Tramp! I shouted, Bloody tramp! He didn't even turn a hair. Wait'll he sees what we've got waiting. You hear that, girly? You hear that, pretty girl?' Daniel didn't move, didn't speak.

Askew leaned over me, gripped Daniel's thigh. 'Such pretty legs,' he growled. 'Such pretty cheeks. You'll get the beast rising.' I stood up and pushed them apart. 'Askew!' I said. But it was too late. The tramp had entered the lane. 'Tramp!' yelled Askew. 'Beast! Look what we've laid out for you.' And he squatted over Daniel, spread him like a sacrifice upon the beach. 'Wouldn't you like this lovely girly boy?' he roared. It made the tramp dead still. He stood before the house and he stared down at us, as if willing us to see the true depths of his exhaustion. Then he turned his face towards the empty sky, opened the red gash of his mouth, and truly like an animal began to howl.

Afterwards, in the silence, Daniel was free. Askew knelt stupidly in the sand, over nothing. The coal gatherers and their ponies had turned to us in wonder. I gripped the photograph, held it tight in my fist. Nothing but the sea moved. There seemed nothing left, but then there came my father, in excitement, yelling from inside,

'Tom...! Tom...! Oh, Tom...!'

INSTEAD OF
THE SCHEME

ALL THAT WEEK, THE WEATHER DIDN'T CHANGE. ON FRIDAY MICKEY just stood there on the doorstep in his shorts, with his overalls slung over his back. I knew he was going to say it again.

'Sod the scheme. Let's go to the beach instead.'

All that week I'd told him no, but this time I shrugged and told him to hang on. I went back in, changed into my trunks, heard my mother coming up after me.

'Come on Rob,' she shouted. 'Don't slip back. Don't waste your good work now.'

I pulled my overalls back on, had to push past her on the stairs.

'Get out there,' she said. 'Move. And get those buttons fastened up.'

We laughed about her as we headed for the Metro, cutting through the back streets to keep out of sight. At Heaton Road we rested and looked through the traffic at the other lads lined up outside the church waiting for Norman to arrive.

'See?' said Mickey. 'See how bloody tame they are?'

I pulled him back into the lanes.

'Bloody right,' I told him. 'Come on, run. You've got to do it, got to break loose sometime.'

We kept going as far as Byker, where all the terraces

had gone, where you could see right out over the city to the bridges and the river and the hills twenty miles away. For once the whole place seemed shining and still, nothing but a gentle roar coming out of it. I held him back, told him to take it in. I wanted to tell him how foreign it was, how different it could be. But we had to run again when we saw the yellow Metro swerving out from underground and coming up the hill.

The Metro was packed. It was the holidays. There were hundreds of children on with their parents. I was shoved into the aisle, but Mickey stayed by the door with space all around him. I saw how people watched him, how they couldn't take their eyes off him, how he just stood there dead calm, as if nothing could ever bother him. 'He's a proud one,' my mother had always said, and it was true. I'd known that from the first time I ever saw him, last year at the start of the scheme. Norman had taken us round the church, told us all the changes that had to be made. He took me aside and whispered, 'Any objection to pairing up with the laddo there?' I looked at the others laid out on the altar steps, passing round the fags, then back at Mickey all alone with the light from the stained glass windows pouring down at him. I shrugged and said he looked all right. 'Good lad,' said Norman. 'I could see you're one with sense.' Then he grinned. 'Don't let him hex you, mind.'

Most people were set to stay on to the coast, but at Wallsend a few men shuffled off for the yards. I squeezed onto a seat beside a man with a huge carrier on his knee, stuffed with towels and food and bottles of home brew. His kids were piled up at the window, staring out. He wanted to talk. He asked where I was working, but when I started to tell him, his little girl started crying and he had to concentrate on calming her down. I laughed with him and just sat back, enjoying rattling along past the cranes on the river, reading the spray on the walls of the old factories – lots of faded writing about the NF and aggro, then the new stuff that started in America or somewhere, beautifully painted cartoons, massive patterns of monsters and heroes, things that must have taken nights and nights to make.

At Tynemouth, walking down towards the Priory, Mickey burst out laughing at me. He tugged my overalls open and held his hand on his eyes as if I dazzled him. Get them off, he told me. I couldn't go onto a beach like that. I was on the loose. Free. He put his hand inside, started to roll the overalls off my shoulders.

'Howay, Rob. Where's your style?'

I felt ridiculous, standing there on the pavement, stripping down to my trunks and trainers. But I had to laugh, and once we were walking again I did start to feel freer, more like him. I told him it was like the dream where you're caught in town with nothing on, and he said aye, he knew that one all right.

We leaned on the blue railings at the bottom of the street. The long beach that stretched north was still deserted, but underneath the Priory dozens of people were already laid out on towels and children were splashing in the water. Everybody knew this was the best beach. With the cliffs all around and the tide going out, it would be like an oven by twelve-o-clock.

We ran down the steps to it. There wasn't a breath of wind down there, and the sea was gentle, just going sh sh as it went out. A smell of coffee and bacon came from the tiny cafe against the cliffs, and closer to the sea we caught the sweet smell of suntan lotion from the girls. We left our things in a heap, ran, dived, and came up hooting at the cold. But you always get used to it, and soon we were swimming across the bay, me practising my strokes, trying to move like I'd been taught at school, so smooth that I hardly made a splash, and Mickey disappearing again and again when he dived to touch the floor. He started to come up under me, pulling me down to the icy cold and dark, where we wrestled in the seaweed before bursting up to the top again. I was worn out when I finally kicked free of him and swam back to the sand. He came out ages later, dripping wet and sparking with the sun behind him, his hands full of tiny shells that he scattered all over me.

We spread out our overalls and lay on them. I kept talking about the church, about what the others would be doing now, trapped in there while we were here. I said,

'Sometimes you want it to be like this. Like nothing else. It lets you see things properly when it's like this.' I used the words I'd heard so many times from him. 'You see how they try to make you something you don't want to be.'

He said nothing.

'Don't you?' I said.

He leaned up, shading his eyes from the sun, and looked at me.

'Aye,' he said. 'They get you slowly, bit by bit.'

Then he lay quiet again with his eyes closed, letting the sun beat down on him. He kept stretching, digging his toes and his fingers into the sand. I watched the white salt showing on his skin as he dried. I watched the tattoo that filled his back. The red eyes were coloured in, and the red tongue, and the black inside its mouth. Different scales were different colours, all the others were his own smooth brown. Lying there beside him in the heat, I could hardly stop myself from tracing the outline, feeling the empty scales and the coloured scales, searching his skin with my spread fingers. 'Mickey,' I whispered after a while, wanting to talk to him and get to know him, but he didn't move and he didn't speak.

I knew them well, these times he went so far into himself it seemed I'd never get him back. They made me understand the other lads, how they'd ask, 'Why do you want to hang about with him? What is he? Nowt but a ponced-up coon with a fancy tongue and a big tattoo. Get rid of him.' Sometimes I thought all that myself, especially on Friday nights when I went down into town with them. 'Where's the coon?' they'd ask, after a few drinks. 'How's the chocolate licking?' But I didn't care. It was great after a week of work to be out there in the crowd, going from bar to bar, looking for girls to take into shop doorways or under bridges. Nights like that, Mickey seemed a world away as if there was, like they said, something twisted in him. It used to worry my mother at first, me coming home drunk in the middle of the night, but my dad understood. He told her to stop fussing. I had to learn. I had to find my way. Saturday mornings I spent flat out in bed with my head throbbing, thinking back to the time we'd had.

I hated it when Mickey came looking for me then. My mother wouldn't let him come upstairs, so I'd go down and stand there on the doorstep with him. 'Out with the lads again, eh?' he'd say. 'Aye, that's the style.' I knew then why the others wanted nothing to do with him, why they used to say, 'He'll get what's coming, mind. Watch out you're not around.'

The tattoo had been coming for months, since just after the scheme started. It was a snake with its tail inside his shorts, its coils all the way up his back, its head high and its mouth open wide at his neck. Every Thursday he went after work to get five pounds worth of it coloured in. The first time we saw it was in April, when the weather started to change. We were in the graveyard with our lunchboxes when he rolled down his overalls. Norman burst out laughing. He'd seen it all, he said. Now he'd seen it all. And how much was that costing, son? Mickey stared at him, then he told him. Norman went on laughing, but I could see the other lads didn't know what to think. They kept looking at the ground, then at each other, like they were waiting for something. It just took one of them to start, and soon they were all giggling like a pack of kids. I tried to catch Mickey's eye, to let him know I wasn't in with them, but he took no notice. He just shook his head and lay down on the grass between the graves, sunbathing. That afternoon Norman told Mickey he was going too far. He was making things worse for himself. Nobody would ever take him on if they got a glimpse of it. Maybe there was a way of getting rid of it. But Mickey laughed right in Norman's face, and boasted about the tiger he'd planned for his chest. When I said Norman might be worth listening to, he bared his teeth at me and said nothing else all day.

All morning they kept streaming down the steps, so many of them you wondered how the beach would ever take them all. But it did take them, with their umbrellas and airbeds and plastic chairs, and we still kept our thin circle of empty sand around us. By lunchtime, it was as if there was some huge party going on. Music was blaring out from radios. Kids kept running past, screaming and kicking up the sand. Outside the cafe two men in sawn-off jeans sat on tall red chairs looking out to sea. They had loudhailers for when anything went wrong, but they just used them for shouting and singing to the crowd. Every few minutes it was Hi de Hi, getting everybody to yell back their Ho de Ho. The air was filled with the smell of food. Packets and boxes were being opened. White cartons and wooden forks were being carried from the cafe. I opened my own box and tapped Mickey's shoulder. 'Dinner break,' I told him, repeating Norman's daily joke, 'Time to hit the tombs,' but he took an age to come round then wanted nothing but to share my orange and get the sea out of his mouth. He peered at the people, amazed to see them all. He cursed at the noise, but he laughed, saying how easy it was to make them pleased, and didn't mean it like he sometimes did.

'I mean, look,' he said, pointing at the man I'd sat with on the Metro. His kids had dug a hole for him, and he was stretched out in it, grinning as they used their little spades to bury him.

'It's all they need, Rob, isn't it? Nothing much, just this.'

'Yes. Good weather. Simple pleasures.'

'Aye. Ha!' He grinned as he picked a pip from his teeth. 'But what the hell, eh? It's just to keep you down. You're allowed a little bit of this, but it's just to keep you down.'

I agreed again, and I started to say something about finding a way of never having to work. But I kept it back. We'd said it all before, and anyway I knew it was different for me than it would ever be for Mickey. I might have broken out today, but I knew I'd learned from the scheme about how places are made and how to fix them. I knew the scheme might work for me and I might somehow get a job through it. I wanted to work. I wanted to get my own place someday and make it fine. But what did Mickey want? Sometimes he seemed so clever you'd think he could do anything. Even Norman said it was Mickey who had the quickest head and the quickest hands. Once I'd watched him strip a stained glass window to its separate parts, clean it up, then reassemble it perfectly. It was wonderful, real craftsman's work. None of the rest of us would have even known where to start. But when I told him that, he just laughed and started to prise out pieces of the glass and sent them skidding across the floor into the rubble. 'Better like that, eh?' he said, looking down at some saint outside a city with little holes all around him. Later he leaned against the wall and watched me hunting for the pieces then forcing them back into place. I was so clumsy I botched the whole thing, twisted the frame, tearing the lead, so it looked hardly any better than when he'd started. That was the first time I swore at him. 'You sod, Mickey. You fucking sod.' But of course he just went on grinning and called me poor lad. I could have strangled him. I saw that even about him and me I didn't know. We'd had nearly a year of working together, but once the year was over and the scheme was done with, there was no way of knowing if I'd ever see him again.

He was watching a girl wading onto the beach. She was tall and thin and her wet hair was clinging to her shoulders. She had a silver chain around her waist and her costume had metal threads in it, making it shine like gold. At the water's edge she sat facing the sea with the water rising and falling across her legs. I watched her with him. She was so beautiful, nearly as brown as he was, as if she'd spent months in another warmer place. And I watched him. I'd not seen him with girls before. He hardly talked about them, not like the other lads, about who he'd had and who he wanted, but I could tell by the way he looked that he wanted her.

It didn't bother him. He just stood up, told me to watch his things, walked down to her. My heart was racing. I was sure she'd send him away. Maybe it was because he did it all without any fuss that she let him sit with her. They talked easily, and were soon making each other laugh. Once she turned, gave me a sudden smile, a wave and I found myself willing her to stay with him, love him. I lay back. Already I could feel my skin beginning to burn. The sun was glaring from above the ruins of the priory and I couldn't look at the sky. I tried to imagine finding a girl for myself, the four of us spending the whole summer together on the beach, getting brown, being free, needing nothing. I tried to lie quiet and still like Mickey had. I heard all the noise dying as if the heat had stunned everyone. Somewhere a woman screeched at her children to shut up, to settle down. I couldn't stand it. I sat forward again, just in time to see Mickey and the girl enter the sea. They were wonderful, Mickey with his bright tattoo and his shorts flapping at his legs, the girl with her tiny gold bikini and the skin between her bottom and her legs creasing and uncreasing as she walked forward. They swam out slowly in a dead straight line from the centre of the beach then turned towards the rocky headland below the priory. Out there the water was like glass. They moved with long smooth strokes, their heads dipping into and out of the water, until they disappeared behind the rocks, and all you could see was their wake.

There was no shade. The few caves in the cliffs already had families in them, squatting around baskets of food and steaming jugs. I waited for a while, but I had to leave. I took my money and my trainers and picked my way over the bodies towards the steps. I climbed slowly, kept stopping to scan the water, but caught no sign of them. At the top a cool breeze was blowing off the land. Outside The Gibraltar Rock men on holiday or on the dole leaned against the walls drinking beer. They wore light clothes with their shirts open wide, and their wives and children sat by them on white chairs beneath umbrellas. Walking past them all towards the door, I knew that if only it could be summer always, the place might still not be grand or rich, but it might be fine, with no problems for anyone.

I drank in the cellar bar, enjoying the moist half-darkness after the hot beach. The first drink hardly touched the sides. I sipped the second, glancing into the mirror behind the bar, smiling at how red my face and shoulders were, but thinking that this might be the beginning of my first real tan. When I went out again I looked and saw the overalls spread out on the sand with nobody near them. I climbed the grassy slope to the priory gates. The notices said that the north had been born in these ancient places. By the time the Vikings came to destroy the buildings, murder the monks and rape the nuns, it was too late to put a stop to everything. From the gates I could see where the river met the sea. On the opposite bank girders were screeching and thumping onto concrete as the warehouses were ripped down. Further in, the cranes were dead still, waiting their turn. Beyond them, I saw nearly as far as Newcastle. I tried to imagine the river and everything I saw with all the workplaces gone. I tried to imagine the past, before Tynemouth, before Newcastle, before any of this, when there were just rough fields and woods along the backs, the roads just dirt and the towns little rings of smoking huts. I tried to see everything lifted away, to see what was underneath it all, like when we had torn out the floor of the church and Norman had said we were looking at ground that hadn't been seen for centuries. But it was too much to deal with. It was easier to look at maps and see all the little crosses spreading out from Tynemouth, Durham, Lindisfarne, taking the whole place over, making it change. I could see it like a pattern then, but I still couldn't take it in, not really.

With no one watching the gate I slipped inside without paying. I expected to see everything laid out, labels everywhere, exhibits displayed in glass cases. I expected to see what our church would be, but on a grander scale. But behind the huge front wall there were just broken archways and bits of stone column and trenches to show where the walls had been. The slopes down to the cliffs were packed with graves worn almost smooth by wind and spray. I saw how perfect it must have seemed here, to have the protection of so many cliffs and so much water, and I saw why they'd chosen this place for the newer buildings at the point – the coastguard station, the low concrete gun emplacement left over from the war. I went right out there and stood above where the guns had been. Behind me, for miles on either side, the shores were crammed. In front, everything was empty, shining, motionless. My whole body was trembling. I felt exposed, all alone, as if I had truly broken free of the scheme and my parents, and I began to tell myself, This is where you start to change and grow. Then my head began to reel and I had to crouch on all fours, collecting myself. That was when I saw them, far below on a tiny stretch of sand. They lay side by side with their few clothes scattered around them. I waved and waved, but they must have been sleeping or keeping out of the glare. I lay for minutes across the concrete waiting for them to wake and move, then I saw that the shadow of the headland would soon reach them. Soon they would go back to the beach. I turned towards the gates again. Walking into the sun, I had to hold the gravestones as I tottered through, knowing that at any moment I could collapse.

Half the beach was in shadow. The sunbathers had shifted closer to the sea. Families were gathering their belongings, coming past me on the steps as I went heavily down, gripping the handrail for support. At the foot I dropped to the sand, leaned on the rock. I must have fallen asleep. I found the little girl in front of me, holding out the overalls.

'Mister. Mister. Dad said give you these, Mister.'

Behind her, the man I'd met that morning waved at me, then he turned and yelled at the water, telling his other children to get out.

'Thank you,' I said, taking the overalls, beginning to pull mine on. My teeth were chattering. I was icy cold

'Not that they'd've got nicked,' he said when he came to us with his packed carrier. Tide'd've got them, though. Look at the little sods. They'll do owt but what they're told.' He looked down at me. I was struggling to fasten the buttons at my throat. And he grinned like my father would, half-amused, half-concerned.

'Been drinking then?' he asked.

'Hardly anything.'

'It doesn't help, though, does it?'

I shook my head.

'You're not used to this, are you? This weather?'

'No'

'Thought not. I watched you all morning, you and your mate. He'll be bad, I thought. He'll be suffering tonight. Here.' He passed me a half-full bottle of lemonade. 'It's what you need. You're all dried out.'

I drained the bottle, but even so I could feel my body wanting more. He laughed.

'That's right. Get it down. Mind you were trying something, wanting to keep up with him.'

I slumped back against the rock. I stared at the sea. He

went and left me, I thought. The sod just left me. The man kept turning to the water, but he didn't move away.

'Inside job?' he said, and when I didn't understand, 'You work inside.'

'Aye. Yes.'

'Not today, though, eh? You couldn't stand it, not when it's like this. You skived off, eh?'

I didn't know whether he was accusing me, or simply passing the time. I tried to laugh and make a joke of it. Sod you, I thought, when he started his yelling again.

'Little buggers. They just please themselves. I don't blame you, kid. Done it meself in me own day. What'd you say you do?'

'We're making a museum.'

'Oh aye?'

'Aye.' I remembered what Norman had said and how he had impressed me so much. 'It'll show our heritage. It'll show what's been done here. It'll have fragments of everything we've achieved.'

He smiled as his little girl tugged at his legs. She kept telling him to come on, come on home.

'Yes, my pet. Everything that's dead, you mean.'

He stared, waiting for me to argue, and when I was silent he looked back to his other children, two boys and another girl, who were trailing slowly across the sand towards us.

'I know,' he said. 'Old pictures. Proggy mats and pitmen's lamps. Bits of ship. The old days. The bloody old days.'

He knelt beside his children when they came. He dried them with a massive towel and rubbed cream into their cheeks and shoulders. He cursed them as he did it, but his hands were so careful with them, so gentle.

'Poor sods,' he said, kissing them each in turn. 'Even the digging won't be left to do. Go on then, up you go.'

He watched them climbing the first flight, then turned his back to them. I couldn't tell whether he was going to attack me or to cry.

'Look, son,' he said, 'I made things. I made things that sailed right out past here. Ships and rigs, setting out. And there'd be hundreds up on that hill there, watching, cheering fit to bust. My work. Cheering my work. Watching it go out. Understand? Aye? You? You're making nothing. A museum? They've got you digging graves. You're chucking it into a hole and wanting to jump in after it yourself.' He crouched and gripped my collar. 'Can you not see it, son? They've even got you talking dead man's talk. Heritage, achievements, what's been done. Well?' He peered into my eyes. 'Well?' I stared back. I could smell the stale home brew on his breath. Sod off, I thought. Get back to bloody mothering your kids. He sighed and let me go, tucked his carrier under his arm. 'Skiving's right, son. Keep out of it.' He started to grin again before he went away. 'And take those off, eh? Your mate's got the right idea. Strip off, swim out, sod it all.'

Hating him, I watched him going up. What did he know? He was past it all, getting old. Redundant. Like my dad had said, the word meant useless. Things were changing, and he was bitter because they'd left him behind. What use was stripping off and swimming out if you wanted to keep up? I watched all the men leaving the beach. They were worn out

by the sun and their children. Their bodies were brown but
their eyes were red with disappointment and too much beer.
They were half-asleep, half-dead. What could I learn from
them when it was them with one foot in the grave?

I bought more lemonade from the cafe and lay outside
waiting. I watched the tide slowly coming up, the shadow
slowly going down. The breeze had turned and I felt colder
and colder. I pulled Mickey's overalls on top of mine. The
men with loudhailers had long ago come down from their
chairs and they sat inside, talking in loud southern voices.
Students, I thought, in cushy summer jobs. I'd give them
something to do. I went to the door and said,

'I think I know somebody that's drowned.'

They looked at me as if I was some kind of freak.

'Two of them,' I said. 'They went out hours ago.'

'I mean it,' I said.

I picked up one of the loudhailers and we went outside,
down to the water's edge. They just stared out stupidly. I
could see they thought I was messing them about. I lifted the
loudhailer to my mouth and said,

'Mickey. Mickey.'

The noise echoed round the cliffs and brought people
running to stand beside us and ask, What's wrong, What's
wrong?

'I mean it,' I said. 'They were on the rocks when the tide
was out. Now there's nowhere for them, and they haven't
come back. So what are you going to do?'

One of them shrugged and pulled off his t-shirt. He
waded into the water and began to swim quickly towards the

headland. While he was out an old woman with a pink rubber hat stretched over her head put her arm on my shoulder. It'd be okay, she told me. The rescue services were wonderful now. When he disappeared I could feel her trembling as she whispered, 'Don't worry, son. It'll all be fine.' As he came back, everyone splashed out to meet him. He came out with his hands held up at the stupidity of it all.

'No problem,' he told me, with a big grin on his face. 'All they said was, Come on out as well.'

He took the loudhailer and went back to the cafe with his friend. I could hear them beginning to roar with laughter. 'You see?' the woman said. 'You see?' Others came to congratulate me, then the crowd dispersed. I cursed them all. I cursed Mickey and I cursed his girl. What do they know? I thought. All this is nothing to do with them. He's from Bangla Desh or somewhere, like his snakes and tigers straight out of the bloody jungle. She'll flaunt herself to some rich git and get him to see to her. They think they're out of it. They think it's all just crap, but what they got that's better? Bloody big tattoos and suntans and gold bikinis. What good's that going to bring them, eh? They know nothing. Nowt. Sod them. Sod them all.

I thought of leaving, but I went on waiting. Miles out, a massive ship steamed south. The tide was bringing in plastic bottles, sandwich wrappings, dead weed. I heard the shutters on the cafe slammed down. I thought of home, my parents expecting me, the trouble there'd be if they found out. I should have gone in, I thought. I might have wasted it all. And what do you do if you waste your chances?

What do you leave yourself?

'Mickey,' I whispered, wanting to scream at him, 'Mickey.'

I took off the overalls and threw them up onto the beach. The water was icy. It took me minutes to get in and once I got started it was like I'd already been swimming for days. I was clumsy and sore and I could see hardly anything for all the splashing I made. I kept thinking I was going under, that I'd have to yell for help. But slowly I rounded the corner to where their beach had been.

The beach was gone. They were higher up now, sitting on a ledge with their arms around each other. I half-swam, half-scrambled from the sea. I tried to shout to them but all I could do was gasp and cough out water. I was climbing towards them when Mickey leaned over, grinned down at me.

'Daft sod,' he said. 'Here, get my hand.'

He hauled me up and they shuffled aside, letting me in, making no move to cover themselves.

'He said you'd come,' she told me. 'I'm glad you did.'

She was smiling at me, and was even lovelier than I remembered. I tried to answer her, but I was useless, embarrassed by her nakedness. I hunched awkwardly at a distance from them, and didn't know where to turn my eyes.

'Fancy sending out the guard,' he said. I could hear the amusement in his voice.

'I waited ages. I thought you'd drowned.'

He laughed. I kept my head turned away from him. I stared at the green moss that covered the ledge, at the rock face that was filled with scratched-in names and dates. I told myself, Get out of this.

'You think too much,' he said. 'Relax. Take your things off.'

'I just came to see you were okay.'

'We're fine. Come on. Nobody can see.'

'No.'

I felt his hand on my arm.

'Come on, Rob.'

I think I'd have left then, just let myself tumble down into the dark water, but the girl suddenly said, 'Leave him, eh?'

She pulled him back towards her. She pushed him until he was lying face down on the moss, and he laughed, letting her. With my face burning I watched as she began to trace with her fingers the long curved outlines of his tattoo. She winked at me.

'Ignore him, Rob. He's just a savage, not like us.'

She started to talk about herself. Her name was Sharon, and she was our age. All the time she talked her fingers moved on him and he laughed softly, shifting from side to side.

'Schemes?' she said. 'I started one as well. They put me in a hospital laundry. Sometimes you had to scrape the shit off the sheets before the machines would take them. Or the guts. I got to hate all those people upstairs, lying down and dying. I kept thinking about the kids back at school, lining up to take my place. We were checked in every morning and out every night. They made you put your hair in nets and your feet in rubber boots. Every Tuesday two jerks with degrees sat on a desk and wanted to know if we knew what johnnies were and which way we wiped our arses. One Friday I took my boots off and chucked them in the machine. They said they understood, they wouldn't get rid of me for that. It was my age, they said. I had to learn to fit in. Fit in a box, they meant. Sod that, I said. I'll have to get rid of myself, then. Bye bye. Sod you.'

'It sounds terrible,' I said, as she giggled at the memory. 'We get nothing like that. Ours is okay.'

Mickey's laughter spluttered at that. 'Oh aye?' he yelled, but she cuffed him and told him to settle down.

'He told me you liked it,' she said.

'It's better than nothing.'

'Aye? But nothing's okay, Rob. Nothing's fine. Sign on, get the giro, go to the beach.'

I shrugged, and looked down at the moss again. Beneath it the water was swelling, slapping the rocks. I was exhausted, and just wanted to leave. So drained, that even my embarrassment was gone, I could get no more pleasure from her beauty.

'Mickey,' she whispered, 'He thinks I'm a waster.'

'No.' I shook my head. 'Sometimes I wish I had the guts to do the same.'

Mickey twisted his head towards me.

'Like hell does he,' he said. 'He's a worker. He thinks it'll all be different for him. Don't you Rob?'

'I don't know. I don't know.'

Sharon leaned across and put her hand on my shoulder.

'It's all right,' she said. 'He told me something else today. He told me how he wished sometimes he was more like you. He told me how he loved you.'

'Watch,' she said, when Mickey was face down again.

'Watch how he shivers when I touch him here.' She giggled as the muscles on his back rippled and the air burst from his mouth. 'See? Go on, try it.'

I hesitated, but she took my hand and put it on him. I let it rest there, then I let my fingers run freely over the brown scales and the coloured scales. I touched the tongue and the teeth and began to follow the coils towards the small of his back. I hesitated again.

'Mickey,' I said, 'What's it like getting this? How much does it hurt?'

'It's nothing. A bit of pain at first, then it's over. Go on. What you stopped for?'

I continued, until the ripples came again and his whole body stiffened.

'Ha!' he said. 'Not bad, but not so good. What's wrong?'

I'd pulled my hand away. I sat shivering with my knees tight on my chest.

'I don't know. Nothing.'

The sea was rocking, sending icy spray at us. The shade was like winter, the moss like frost.

'I shouldn't have come. I won't be able to get back.'

They were both on their knees. I glared at them.

'I won't,' I said. 'I won't.'

I said, 'You bastard, Mickey. You've ruined everything.'

I tried to pull away, but she reached out again, put her hands flat against me.

'You're freezing,' she said. 'Sunstroke. You were out too long. Come here. Come on in.'

She pulled me gently, and they shifted apart, letting me

crawl between them.

'That's right,' said Mickey. 'That's better. You'll be fine now. Just relax.'

They put their arms around me and came in close. When they felt how wet my trunks were, they helped me off with them. I felt their heat, their gentleness. I tried to tell Mickey how sorry I was, but he just said no, don't worry, it was nothing. We lay an age like that, watching the sea and sky change colour, sometimes whispering about the day it had been. Soon my body changed, stopped trembling. I found myself thinking of the overalls turning in the waves, my parent's rage, the lads gathering in the town, but all I could do was smile. Lying there under the priory with nothing on, being warmed by Mickey and his girl, I knew that I'd be able to get back, that everything would be fine, that till the sun went down there was nowhere else I'd rather be.